Blood In

GREEN SWAMP

BY

D.L. BURRIS

ALTHOUGH SOME PLACES MENTIONED IN THIS BOOK ARE REAL THIS BOOK IS ENTIRELY FICTION

CHAPTER 1

Visitors to Oak Island soon learn the place to be at sunset is not on the beach, but on the high-rise bridge that connects the island to the main land. There you will see a sunset that will compete with any in the world. While Key West gets all the publicity, Oak Island has remained a hidden treasure. There is even a small town nearby named for the sunset, Sunset Harbor. On down the coast Sunset Beach is also named for the beautiful sunset.

Oak Island is the largest of North Carolina's southern barrier islands. Instead of facing the ocean on the East Side like all the other barrier islands, Oak Island faces the ocean on the south side. This twist of geography allows a great view of the eastern and western sky from anywhere on the island. Early risers find the sunrise to be as spectacular as the sunset. Though larger then the other barrier islands, Oak Island is only eleven miles long and two miles wide. It consists of summer homes, a few motels, and various retail stores. There's also a nice marina where boats going up and down the waterway can gas up or moor their boats for the night. With the Atlantic Ocean on one side and the Intracoastal Waterway on the other, the bridge is the only tie between the island and the main land. The bridge is fairly new and modern. It is built out of concrete instead of steel. Concrete can withstand salt water and salty mist much better than steel. It is high enough for the tallest sailboat to go under. High-rise bridges are fast replacing the old fashion drawbridges all along the coast. These bridges allow large boats to travel the waterway without interfering with auto traffic. The first time you cross a high-rise bridge can be a real test of nerves. You can't see over the top of the bridge, so it looks like you'll drop right off into the water. When you reach the top, instead of dropping, off you're treated to a magnificent view. You can see the whole island from the top of the Oak Island high-rise bridge.

Visitors find the island to be a nice escape from the outside world, a world unto itself. Calm and laid-back is the norm. Once you experience the serene atmosphere, it stays in your head like a favorite song. You return over, and over, and over again. It's the perfect place to break away from the rat race world. If you just want to relax this is the place to be. While most other beaches are over crowded and over commercialized, Oak Island reminds you of the beach in the fifties. Practically all of the homes are used as summer vacation homes. The island is booming during the summer tourist season, and like a ghost town during the winter. There are less than a thousand year round residents. Most of them make a living from the ocean one way or another. The year round residents, or locals as they prefer to be called, are like one big family. They have that old fashioned togetherness that is missing in so much of our world. Of course the problem with that is everyone knows everything about everybody else. Things are changing fast though. For the past couple years or so the island, and the inland area next to it, have been one of the fastest growing areas in the nation. Older folks from up north have found the island to be a great place to retire. With it's mild winters and breezy summers the islands weather draws people from snow country like a magnet. With the exception of those who make a living from real estate or tourism the local population hate to see the area change. They have no desire to see their island overrun with people all year. Most of them think it's far to crowded in the summer already. They long for the good old days when all the barrier islands were relatively unheard of. As far as they're concerned all the so-called progress has ruined their way of life. If they wanted to live at a beach that was overrun with people, and had bumper-to-bumper traffic, they would move to Myrtle Beach, South Carolina. It's only forty miles to the south. People flock to Myrtle Beach for the variety of things to do there. People come to Oak Island to sit back and do nothing.

Police chief Steve Holder, three deputies, and two dispatchers are the complete law enforcement on the island. Chief Holder spent twenty-five years in the Army Military Police. He is originally from Dallas, Texas. He spent many years stationed at North Carolina's, Fort Bragg. There he met his wife, a cute, sweet, and petite little thing, named Lilly. Lilly might have been petite when they got married, but you could hardly call her that today. Being married to a career military man is a very stressful life. She thought Steve's retirement would end the stress, but since he became Chief of Police, it's as bad as ever. Her remedy for fighting stress has always been to eat junk food. Let's just say that after twenty years of marriage she's put on a few pounds.

The Holder's always vacationed on Oak Island each summer, and both of them fell under its spell. When he retired from the Army, the pull of the island was strong, so they moved there for better or worse. Four years ago the old police chief retired and Holder got the job. Steve in only fifty years old, so he figures he can work for ten more years. After that he plans to retire to a life of leisure. Actually he enjoys being chief so much it doesn't seem like work. He runs the department with the same authority he commanded in the military. Two of his deputies, Jim Walker, and Bobby Young, are locals, the third deputy; John Martin is from the nearby town of Southport.

Crime is not a big problem on Oak Island. A few fender benders and bar fights, especially during tourist season. With only one way on or off the island, traffic in general can be a big headache. Every now and then some brave soul will leave his brain on the bus and break into a summer house, but all in all life is good on Oak Island. There is a mutual respect between the locals and the police. Outsiders cause Ninety per cent of the islands crime problems.

Steve is the perfect representation of a protector of the people. He stands six foot four inches tall and all of his one hundred eighty pounds are pure muscle, not an ounce of body fat in sight, compliments of the Army's discipline. He seems calm and laid back but the local folks know better. He will not take crap from anyone, especially low-life crooks and degenerates. He has a way with words that leaves no doubt he is in charge. His eyes are a clear hypnotic blue that turns to cold steel when he is pissed. His eyes are about to get very, very cold

It is early October; four o'clock on a Thursday morning, and deputy John Martin is on patrol. He has just pulled into Mike's Service Station, which is the only place that stays open twenty-four hours this time of the year.

"How's the coffee," he asked.

"It's really good," answered Mary "I just made a new pot around midnight. I've only sold a few cups since then, so there should be plenty of it in the pot. I'm having a cup myself, got to do something to stay awake."

Mary was Mike Steel's wife. She worked the night shift while Mike worked the daytime shift, so he would be there when most of the car repair business was needed.

"It's been awful slow since tourist season is winding down," said Mary "we'll probably start closing at midnight after this month. No need staying open if we don't have any customers. I don't mind telling you I'm a little afraid being here by myself all night. Thank God we got you guys riding by to check on things, but I know you've got the whole island to cover by yourself. You've got too much to do to worry about just me."

"We'll look after you," answered Martin "I can't recall anybody ever robbing a store on the island anyway. This place is safe even in the middle of the night."

"I ought to be here in the daytime anyway. Mikes so busy working on people's cars we have to pay somebody to run the cash register. We'd do about as well to just close at night. I could be at home in a nice warm bed now."

"Then were would I get my coffee," laughed Martin "it's pretty boring on night shift now too, I haven't passed a car in two hours. It's a lot different from when all the tourist were here. Then we'd have people driving around all night long. We still get a good crowd on weekends through. People will keep coming until the weather turns to cold and the fish stop biting."

"That's true," answered Mary "we still get enough customers on weekends to make it worth staying open all night, but during the week there's not enough for me to lose sleep over."

"Mary you sure do make a good cup of coffee," replied Martin "it's just what I need to keep me awake. Let me have a couple jelly doughnuts to go, I better get back on patrol, it's time to check the bridge."

"I don't see why," laughed Mary "nobody's going to be using it at this time of the morning."

"It's worth coming in here just to hear your sarcastic remarks," replied Martin. Martin left the store and drove toward the bridge. He was just about at the top of the high-rise bridge when something caught his attention. He slowed down and turned on his spotlight. There in the inbound lane sat a car. Martin turned around, pulled behind the car, and turned on the blue lights. It was a late model white BMW. The first thing he noticed was that the license plate was missing. What the hell is this he thought. He got on his radio and called the dispatcher.

"You're not going to believe this, but I just found a car setting at the top of the bridge."

"You're right," replied the dispatcher "that's hard to believe. What kind of car is it?"

"It's a white BMW. It can't be more than two years old."

"Do you see the driver anywhere?"

"No, I don't see anybody."

"Give me the license plate number, and I'll run it through the computer."

"There ain't no license plate on it. I'm going to check it out."

"OK, just be careful, and radio back as soon as you can."

With his pistol in one hand and a flashlight in the other, Martin approached the vehicle. The driver's window was rolled down, the car was empty, but the keys were in the ignition. Martin walked all the way around the car. Outside the fact that here was an empty vehicle, in the middle of a bridge, at four in the morning, he saw nothing out of the ordinary. Where was the driver? Had he or she jumped off the bridge? He checked under the left side of the windshield for a vehicle identification number; there was none. He was careful not to touch anything; the car would have to be checked for fingerprints. He looked over the edge of the bridge. Between the darkness and the height of the bridge, he could only make out murky, black water below. He went back to his car and called the dispatcher.

"This is weird as hell. There's no one around here. There's no license plate or vehicle identification number on the car. I don't know how we're going to find out who owns it. You'd better transfer me to the chief. I hate to wake him up at this time of the morning but he needs to see this for himself. He's the pro at getting fingerprints anyway."

It's a little after four in the morning and Chief Holder is being rudely awakened from a sound sleep by Martin's call. It seems that some stupid dipstick has left his new BMW parked on the bridge.

"I know crime is at low tide now John, but can't you figure out all by your little lonesome what the hell to do," replied the chief.

"Very funny chief, but this is serious. Something is wrong. The window is down and the key is in the ignition. It looks like someone stopped to take a whiz and the gators got him. It's weird, I've got a very bad feeling about this one, or I wouldn't call you at this time of the morning. You better come and see this for yourself. You need to check it out before I call Mike to bring the wrecker."

"Aw shit! Its probability some yuppie tourist thinking the locals are so ignorant that no one would think to drive away in his yuppiemobile, so he went to take a piss and got his ass lost. You did the right thing calling me though. I'll be there in a few minutes so don't touch anything."

"Now I know why you are the chief of police, nothing gets by you."

"You got that right, nothing ever gets by me, and I will definitely remember your tender words of praise on payday. No one can accuse you of being a brown nose, can they John. Want to rephrase that remark?"

"Sorry chief, I'm just excited to have a possibility of a real crime for a change instead of fender benders, bar-fights, and chicken thieves. I think something bad has happened out here. I've got an eerie feeling just standing out here by myself. You know I don't scare easily, but this is a downright spooky situation."

"Go ahead and have the dispatcher call Mike, and get the wrecker out there," answered the chief "we need to move that car as soon as we check everything out. We can't have it blocking the bridge."

Martin called the dispatcher, then stood beside the BMW and waited for the chief. He knew it wouldn't take long; Holder only lived about a mile from the bridge. Twenty minutes later Holder pulled his patrol car in front of the BMW. He left his headlights shining on the BMW, grabbed his flashlight, and walked over to Martin.

"What the hell you got here John?"

"Somebody left their car here and just vanished. I don't know if they jumped or whatever. This is exactly how I found it," answered Martin "I haven't touched anything, maybe we'll find some prints on it."

Holder checked around and under the car. Then he stuck his head through the open window. Satisfied with his initial inspection he said "OK, let's check the door first then we'll get a better look inside."

The chief got out some fingerprint powder and sprinkled some on the door handle.

"No prints here," he said, "let's open the door and get the keys. I want to look in the trunk."

He checked the keys and around the trunk for prints but nothing showed up.

"OK" said the chief "let's open her up."

There were at least ten keys on the ring. Martin tried several before one opened the trunk. Both officers expected to find a body, some dope, or some clue to the car's owner inside. The only thing they found was a spare tire in a pristine trunk.

"Nobody keeps a trunk this clean. There's no dirt, trash, or tools, just the tire. Every body has something in there, even if just an old gum wrapper, cash register receipt, or a dead cat, just something, " speculated Chief Holder. "Hell, it looks like it was just driven off the showroom floor. Either we are dealing with a prize annul retentive son of a bitch, or somebody wants us to think so. Frankly, something about this whole mess just stinks."

"Like I said, nothing gets by you," remarked Martin

"Shut the hell up before I fire your ass! Lets gets this Beamer to the impound so we can give her a good going over. I think you finally have a chance to do some real police work for a change Martin. The first thing we've got to do is find out who the driver was. It's easy to assume that he or she jumped off of the bridge, but we'll still have to do some investigating. With any luck we'll find a body when it gets light."

Just then as if right on cue Mike Steel drove up in his wrecker. The chief got in his car and moved it out of Mike's way. Then he walked over to the wrecker.

"Hook her up and take her to the impound lot," he told Mike "just don't touch anything you don't have to, we've still got to check the rest of it for prints. I don't think we'll find any though. It looks like everything's been wiped clean. Somebody went to a lot of trouble to make sure we couldn't know who was driving that car."

Mike hooked up the BMW and headed for the lot, leaving the chief and Martin standing on the bridge. They both took their flashlights and looked over the side of the bridge. The bridge was so high there wasn't much chance of seeing anything but water in the dark.

"John you've lived around here all your life," said Holder "you ever hear of anybody jumping off of this bridge?"

"No" answered Martin "but it would sure be a good way to commit suicide. Ever now and then somebody in Wilmington will commit suicide by jumping off a bridge but not out here. I don't see why anyone would clean their car up, and take the plate and VIN off if they were going to kill themselves. Why would they go to all that trouble?"

"I don't know," said the chief "it seems kind of nuts, but people planning to take their life can think up some crazy things. You check around both ends of the bridge, maybe the driver's passed out on the bank or something. Stay out here until it gets light, and check the water under the bridge again. I'm going to catch Mike before he leaves."

The chief got in his car and drove away. He pulled into the impound lot just as Mike was unhooking the BMW.

"Before you leave I need you to get the engine ID number," he told Mike "it'll take a while, but we'll find out who owns this heap."

While Mike was getting the ID the chief checked the glove compartment for prints, just as he figured there were none. Then he opened the compartment, no big surprise, it was empty.

It was well past daylight when Martin came in. Of course, he had found nothing at either side of the bridge or in the water. They checked over the rest of the car for prints and found nothing. Whoever that car belonged to had sure done a good job cleaning it up. It didn't make sense unless somebody wanted to keep his or her identity a secret for a while. Holder called the State Bureau of Investigation at Wilmington and gave them the engine ID. Their computers would eventually find out who owned the BMW. Next he called Ron White, the head of the local rescue squad.

"Ron" he said "some dip shit left his car on top of the bridge this morning. I think we've got a suicide. We looked in the water and around the bank the best we could. We didn't even see a clue of where the driver might be. Have some guys patrol the waterway, and see if they find a body or anything suspicious. There's no tag or prints on the car. It's the weirdest thing I've ever seen. I'm trying to find out whom it belongs to, so we'll know who we're looking for. If the car's owner wasn't driving it they should at least know who was. Then I've got to see about finding their next of kin."

“If the driver jumped off of that bridge, there's not much chance he or she survived,” replied White “what time did you find the car?”

“John found it about four this morning.”

“You know the tide was going out about then. If somebody got in that current they might be way out in the ocean by now, if the sharks didn’t eat them first. I’ll send a boat out, and we’ll check around. Don‘t hold your breath waiting for us to find a body though, there might not be anything left to be found.”

“Thanks” said the chief “I agree, we may never find a body but we have to try. Just like I‘m trying to find out who the car belongs to. This is the part of my job I hate. There‘s never an easy way to tell somebody‘s love ones that they‘re dead. Especially when it‘s a suicide.”

“You and I are getting to old for the jobs we’re doing,” replied Ron “maybe we should retire and sit on the beach fishing all day.”

“Right now that’s a very tempting offer,” answered the chief.

CHAPTER 2

An escape from the outside world, clam, and laid back, serene atmosphere, Oak Island sounds like paradise, but there is trouble in paradise. When something as strange as a car is found abandoned on top of the only connection between the island and land, lots of questions are asked. By noon most of the locals had heard about the car, and they were asking all sorts of questions. Who did the car belong to? Who was driving it? Why would anyone pick that bridge to commit suicide? Why would they clean up the car and take the license plate off? Lots of people went by the impound lot and looked at the car. Nobody could recall ever seeing if before. That just made the whole thing more curious. Why would a stranger come to their island and commit suicide? Chief Holder assured everyone he'd soon know who owned the car. He also predicted the rescue squad would find a body, or at least parts of a body. There was soon a line of people on top of the bridge. Everyone wanted to see where all the action had taken place. Lots of them had binoculars, searching over the waterway, hoping they'd be the one to spot a body. They thought they could see more from the top of the bridge than the rescue squad could see patrolling the waterway. Since this was near the end of the tourist season most of the locals had plenty of time on their hands. Hours spent on the bridge, looking for a body, sure beat setting at home watching TV. After a full day searching from the boat and bridge nothing had been found. Ron White told Chief Holder he would search again early the next morning. He reminded the chief that with all the sharks feeding there might not be a body left to be found.

Even in paradise there are some secrets. Oak Island has some big secrets. A particular crime has been carried out on the island for a long time. If the cops and local residents knew what was happening, and who was doing it, they would be totally shocked. What's that phrase real estate people use: location, location, and location. Oak Island is the perfect location for certain kinds of crime. The kind of crimes that sometimes turn deadly. Oak Island is also located ten miles from a very large swamp. What in the world could that have to do with the car on the bridge? Go back approximately two months before the cops find the car on the bridge. Two brothers were just trying to make some extra money, but they got more than they bargained for. Whether these guys were naive or just plain stupid one thing for certain: people would die.

On the waterway side of the island there are numerous small canals that go right behind peoples homes. Every house has a pier that leads to the canal. People can fish and catch crabs right in their back yards. Boats use these canals just like a highway. The canals take you to the waterway and the waterway takes you to the ocean. There is a navigable inlet on each end of the island. The northern inlet is the mouth of the Cape Fear River. It is also the shipping lane for merchant ships going to the state port at Wilmington and military ships going to Sunny Point Army Depot. In the summertime there are so many boats the canals and waterway resemble Interstate 95, especially on weekends. Small boats have one strict rule. When the big ships are coming in or out, stay far away from them. Their wake is much larger than you think it will be. Ever now and then a small boat will get caught in that wake and either be capsized or sucked under. To the locals these boat drivers are known as weekend idiots. They come to the beach untrained and unprepared for the ocean's strong currents and high waves. They think driving a boat in the ocean is just like driving on the lake back home. Most of them don't even know the difference between a red and green channel marker. If they survive the waves it's not uncommon to find them stuck on a sand bar in the middle of the inlet. That's a funny thing about ocean inlets; places where you'd think the water would be very deep may have a sandbar just below the surface. If a boater is not familiar with the inlet he'd better always stay within the channel markers until he gets past the breakers.

On the northern end of the island is a small canal that goes behind a single house. It is an older house made of brick not like the new houses that set on pillars. You can just look at the size of the lot and tell the house has been there a long time. The lot is three times as big as the new ones, and it has lots of trees. New lots are just big enough for a house and have houses on each side. If their owners are lucky they'll have a tree or two. Real estate people make all the money they can off of the limited space of the island. If people want privacy they have to put up a fence between them and their neighbor.

Ray Cook and his brother Joe live in the house. Ray owns a small shrimp trawler, the Carolina. Joe is first mate on a merchant ship, the Emerald Thai. The Emerald Thai is less than ten years old. It has been equipped with all the newest marine technology. The ship hauls clothing from Thailand to the state port at Wilmington.

Wilmington is the largest city along the North Carolina coast. It is located twenty-five miles north of Oak Island.

It takes about a month to cross the ocean and about a week get to port and load the ship. Then it's another month to return and a week or so to unload the ship. Joe is only home for about a week every two months. Joe was smart enough to graduate from the Merchant Marine Academy, while Ray stayed home and helped their father on the boat. Their mother died from breast cancer while they were both young. Four years ago their father died from stomach cancer. Maybe cancer ran in their family, all their aunts and uncles had died from it. Ray and Joe are the last of their family left on the island. Maybe that was the reason the brothers had a special bond between them. They resemble each other so much they are often mistaken for twins. Both are five ten and have sandy brown hair. Both are in excellent physical condition. There's not the slightest bulge around the middle on either of them. Ray gets plenty of exercise working on the boat, and Joe has a work out room on the ship. Ray is twenty-seven and Joe is a year older. Since Joe had a good job, the old man left the shrimp boat to Ray and the house to both boys. Obviously Ray is there alone most of the time.

The Carolina is fifteen years old, but it's in very good condition. It is made of solid wood with two diesel engines for power. The center of the boat is one big hole where the fish and shrimp are kept on ice. Ray mostly goes after shrimp, but if the fish are running and the shrimp aren't, he'll catch a net full of fish. That's why the Carolina is sometimes referred to as a fishing boat. Ray knows the waters around Oak Island like the back of his hand. He never worries about getting lost or stranded on a sand bar. He takes very good care of the boat. He keeps it as clean as possible and makes sure its engines are serviced on schedule. The last thing he wants is to break down with a boat full of fish or shrimp. Ray loves working on the boat, but it's a rough life. Running a fishing boat is really more of a job than one man can handle. There's just not enough money for him to hire anyone full time. He's hoping everything will soon change. If all his plans work out he won't have to run the Carolina much longer.

Ray was getting the Carolina ready to go out to sea the next day. It was time for Joe to return and he had been waiting for him to call. Around three o'clock his cell phone rang.

"Hello" said Ray

"Hello Ray, it's me," answered Joe "the ships at the two mile buoy, we're suppose to go to port at noon tomorrow."

"Ok, I'll pick you up around noon," said Ray "did you have a good trip?"

"Yes," answered Joe "we had a very good trip. Everything went exactly like it was suppose to. The special cargo will be in the usual place."

"That's great," replied Ray "I'll see you tomorrow."

Ray went back to work on the boat. He had a deal with a seafood company in Wilmington to use one of their refrigerated trucks. He backed the refrigerated truck up right beside the Carolina. Then he shoveled enough ice from the truck to cover the bottom of the boat's hole. It would keep his shrimp fresh the next day. When he didn't have the refrigerated truck he had to stop by the local seafood warehouse and buy ice. The smell in the boat's hole was awful but that smell served a surprising purpose. When he was satisfied with the boat he went in the house, took a shower and went to bed. He would ride out to the two-mile buoy in the morning. It was very important that he be there before sunup.

Ray got up at three the next morning. He ate a light breakfast and filled a big thermos full of coffee. Then went out to the Carolina and cranked her engines up. He eased the Carolina out of the canal, into the waterway, up to the shipping lane, and out to sea. He would be the first trawler out that day, but he wouldn't fish until after sunup. He headed for the two-mile buoy. It was a very clear night and he had no trouble spotting the Emerald Thai. He pulled the Carolina beside the buoy and dropped anchor. The night was so clear he probably wouldn't have to use his spotlight. He studied the ocean all around the buoy. Before long he saw an image of white just below the ocean's surface. He took a long gaff and retrieved the image. He knew what it was, a five-kilo waterproof package held in place by strong fishing line and a ten-pound weight. He carried the package into the boat's hole. Then he shoveled the ice away from the center of the hole. Next he took his screwdriver and removed four screws from the boat's floor. The Carolina is all wood with a treated plywood floor. He removed a small section of floor and put the package on the boat's hull. Then he replaced the floor and covered it back with ice. He went back to the top and cranked up the boat's engines. Then he moved the Carolina about a mile from the ship and got his nets ready. It would be daylight soon, and he would just be another trawler trying to catch some shrimp. There was a good chance the Coast Guard would be patrolling the waterway when he went in, but he wasn't worried. Not even their best dog was going to smell anything in the Carolina's hole. Even if he didn't net many shrimp, the Coast Guard would have no reason to check under the ice in the boats hole.

CHAPTER 3

As the sun raised Ray lowered his nets and trawled the ocean parallel to the shore. He poured a cup of coffee and began to think about how his life had changed the last couple of years. It was a long story, and it seemed like he thought about it every time he went fishing. It all began about a year after his father died. His father always sold his fish and shrimp at the local seafood dealer. Ray had heard from some other fishermen about a dealer in Wilmington that paid a better price. He tried the new dealer and found it was worth the drive if he had a big catch. W & W seafood was the company's name. It was located in an old tobacco warehouse. The back of the building had a roll up door big enough for a truck to drive through it. There is a regular sized door beside the large door for drivers to exit after they have brought their trucks in. Trucks full of seafood could drive inside the building and stay parked overnight. Since all the trucks were refrigerated the seafood would stay fresh. A man named Amos Black ran the company. Black was a likeable fellow, big, and jolly, somewhere in his mid fifties. He had to weight over three hundred pounds, though maybe only five eight in height. He was kind of funny looking. The top of his head was bald with a little hair going all the way around the sides. His legs seemed too small to support all the weight they had to carry around. His face was much larger at the bottom than at the top. His massive jaws resembled those on a hog. There was something about his eyes that made him seem distant; he never looked directly at you when he spoke. Ray had a feeling there was something sinister behind the jolly act. Ray often talked to him while his catch was being unloaded and weighted. He told him about growing up on the island, and about working on the boat with his father. He also told him how proud he was of his big brother and about Joe's ship the Emerald Thai. Sometimes he complained about how hard it was making a living running a fishing boat. Black said he was well aware of that fact; he used to run a boat too. He had also worked on a merchant ship for a few years. Black knew a lot about ships. The last couple of trips it seemed like Black was asking more questions about Joe and what he did on the cargo ship. He seemed particularly interested in the fact that Joe worked twelve hours on night shift and was the only one awake at night while the ship was waiting to come to port. He was also very interested in exactly where in Thailand Joe's ship went to port. Finally on one trip Black invited Ray into his office, handed him a beer, and told him to have a seat.

"Ray" he said, "I want your promise that this conversation stays between you and me. If you can't promise me that, I'll let you drink your beer and be on your way."

"Sure" answered Ray "you got my promise, I never was one to run off at the mouth anyway. Whatever you say is safe with me."

"Ok" said Black "understand this, if this conversation ever leaks out the consequences will be bad, very bad. I'm not joking around, if this information gets out it could cost you your life."

"Keep talking," said Ray "like I said, I'm not going to tell anybody, anything."

“OK” replied Black “I just wanted to make sure we understood each other. I have a business deal for you and Joe, you can make a lot of money, but it’s not legal. I can get some coke to Joe in Thailand, and I have a way worked out for him to get it into the states. I guarantee you we can get by the Coast Guard and DEA. It won’t be much coke, but it doesn’t take a lot to make some good money. That’s all I’m going to tell you now. Talk it over with Joe, and if both of you are interested bring him by here the next time he’s in port. If you’re not interested, this conversation never took place.”

“Wow! I wasn’t expecting anything like that. No wonder you wanted to be sure I never repeated it. Joe will be home in two weeks; I’ll have to talk it over with him then. I’ll let you know one way or the other. I’ve got to admit you’ve certainty gave me a lot to think about. How much money are we talking about?”

I’m not going to give you any numbers today, but I guarantee you it’ll be worth your time and effort. I’ll be expecting to hear from you in two weeks. Then if you and Joe are interested, I’ll tell you everything. Just remember to keep your mouth shut. You can talk it over with Joe, but nobody else.”

Two weeks later Ray was in Wilmington to pick up Joe. Instead of heading home he drove to a park by the ocean. He explained his conversation with Black and said he would let Joe make the final decision.

“I’m getting tired of spending so much time at sea,” said Joe “if we could make some good money I could soon quit. I don’t like the ideal of breaking the law, but let’s go hear what Black’s got in mind. If we don‘t like it we‘ll just say no.”

Ray called Black on his cell phone and was told to come on over to his office. Half an hour later they walked into Black’s office and sat down.

“It’s good to see you Ray,” said Black “so I’m finally getting to meet your big brother.”

“That’s right,” answered Ray “this is Joe”

“Nice to meet you,” said Black “well I suppose this means you are interested in my business deal.”

“Tell us what you have in mind,” said Joe “you have our word that nothing you say will ever be repeated. If we don‘t like your plan we‘ll never talk about it again.”

“That’s exactly what I wanted to hear,” replied Black “Ok, listen up, I’ve thought about this a long time, and I’m sure it will work. Joe while your ship is being loaded in Thailand you pack a heavy suitcase and spend a few days at the beach. Check in the Paradise Motel, it‘s only about a mile from the port. I’ll give you a number to call when you get there, just tell the person on the phone your name and room number. The person on the phone will tell you what time he’ll come to your motel room. He’ll bring you a five-kilo waterproof package and a ten-pound weight. Put them in the suitcase and carry them back on the ship. You don’t have to worry about the cops over there; they’re paid to look the other way. You like to fish, so you will keep a heavy duty-fishing reel loaded with one hundred pound line in your room. Make sure you drop a line in the ocean every now and then so nobody will get suspicious. I used to work on a ship, so I know there is a hatch on top of the ships fuel tank. Tie some line around the package and weight and drop them in the fuel tank. There’s no way the Coast Guard will ever find the coke in there. Ray told me you work the twelve hours on the night shift while the captain works the twelve hours on day shift. That will give you plenty of opportunities to get the coke on and off the ship. I’ve got something for you to take on board; it’s a matching set of bookends. These bookends are really two twenty-pound magnets. When you get to the two-mile buoy your ship has to wait a day or two before it can come to port. That's when you always call Ray and tell him when to pick you up. Tie one of the magnets to some fishing line and get the package out of the fuel tank. The ship has all the newest technology so you'll know how deep the water is. Tie on enough line to keep the package just below the surface. Then throw the weight and package toward the buoy. Ray, you take your boat and pick up the package before daylight. It has to be before daylight, nobody can see you get the package out of the water. We'll have to time our delivery and pick up time close together so the tide won't affect things.

Black turned toward Joe, "I'm thinking you can throw the package in the water two hours before daylight and Ray can pick it up one hour before daylight. Ray, I'll show you how to make a compartment in your boat that the Coast Guard will never find. You'll put the coke in the hidden compartment and cover it up with ice. I know how bad it stinks in the boat's hole; even a dog is not going to smell anything down there. After you've got the coke on board move your boat away from the ship, and catch shrimp like you normally do. With the ice and shrimp on top of the package there's no way the Coast Guard will ever find it. We'll also build a compartment in one of my trucks so you can bring the coke here. After it gets here you guys are finished with it. I'll handle everything from there on. I'm willing to pay you twenty thousand dollars for every package you bring in."

"Wow" said Joe "that's a lot of money, but it's also a very complicated plan. We'll be taking a hell of a risk."

"We sure will," said Ray "I ain't never even had a speeding ticket, but we could spent the rest of our lives in prison if we get caught bringing in dope."

"I'll be taking a lot of risk to," answered Black "I could get caught just like you guys could. That's the reason I want to keep everything on a small level. I don't want any attention at all. You guys will have to make sure you don't throw a lot of money around. Just continue living the way you do now, and put the money away for the future. Remember there's a Coast Guard Station on the island and some of the personnel live there. You sure don't want to make any of them suspicious. Joe the big question is, can you get the package in the fuel tank, and off the ship without anyone seeing you?"

"Sure" answered Joe "I'm the only one awake at night while we're waiting to come to port. I can put it in the tank my first night back on board. Most of the crews still our partying then anyway. Everyone will be asleep when I get it out and throw it in the ocean.

"Ok" said Black "you guys have any questions?"

Ray replied, "let me be sure I understand everything. Some guy in Thailand gives Joe a waterproof package full of coke and a ten-pound weight. Joe ties heavy fishing line around the dope and weight, and drops them in the ship's fuel tank. While he's waiting to come to port at the two-mile buoy he ties a magnet on the end of fishing line and gets the package out. Then he ties enough fishing line between the weight and package to barely keep the package under water. Next he throws the weight and package toward the two-mile buoy. Of course he'll do that at night. Then while it's still dark I pick up the package. Next I hide it in the bottom of my boat in a hidden compartment under the ice and shrimp. If the Coast Guard ever checks me even their dogs won't be able to smell anything in the boat's hole. It smells like hell down there. When I come out of there I stink so bad I have to shower with Clorox and a Brillo pad to scrub the smell off. Then I move the package from the boat to a hidden compartment in one of your trucks and cover it with ice and shrimp. Then I just drive it to your place, and I'm finished with it. That's when you pay us the twenty thousand"

"That's right, that's all you have to do," answered Black "I'll still buy your shrimp like always."

"Well Joe, I said I'd let you make the final decision," replied Ray "what do you want to do?"

"Let's do it Ray," said Joe "it won't take long to save a lot of money, then we can do what ever we want to. I don't want to spend all my life on a ship."

Ray replied, "before we answer let's be sure of one thing, what happens if we decide to quit?"

"If it looks like we're going to get caught we'll all stop," answered Black "I don't want to go to jail any more than you guys do."

"OK" said Ray "you've got a couple of business partners."

That's how the brothers got in the dope business. Everything had worked well for over two years. Although the Coast Guard had checked the ship several times they had found nothing. The Coast Guard seldom bothered with the local fishing boats. A few times they had checked Ray under the pretense of a safety inspection, but he knew they were really looking for dope. A couple of times they even brought a dog on board. There was no way he could smell anything hid in the boat's hole. Amos Black had been true to his word; the money was very good. The brothers were careful not to live beyond their means. The island locals were like a family, everybody knew everybody else. When all the tourist were gone, they had plenty of time on their hands. People were always eager for some new gossip. They knew Joe made good money, they also knew about what Ray made. Nobody gets rich running a fishing boat. Actually the brothers had saved all the money they made from Black. They knew they had been pushing their luck for a long time. Eventually they would get caught. When they had brought in the last load they told Black they wanted to quit after the fishing season was over. They had both found girlfriends and wanted to take them away and start over. Black didn't say anything, but they both knew he wasn't happy.

Ray had caught a nice load of shrimp by ten o'clock. With the catch lying on top of the ice in the boat's hole he wasn't worried about the Coast Guard finding the package. It was time to go in, take his shrimp to Wilmington, collect the money for the dope, and pick up Joe.

He pulled in his nets and headed for home. The waterway was busy now, lots of boats going fishing, and just riding around. It took twice as long to go in as the trip out had taken, but that was ok, he was just another fishing boat. Finally he pulled up to his pier and tied the Carolina off. The refrigerated truck was already as far back as it could go. He would carry his catch from the boat to the truck in a large plastic bucket. Ray climbed down into the boat's hole. He took his shovel and moved the shrimp and ice away from the middle. Then he took his screwdriver, removed the centerboard, and took out the package. The package went in the bucket first, and then it was covered with ice and shrimp. He carried the bucket to the truck, opened the back door, and got in. The truck's hidden compartment was similar to the boats, located right in the center of the bed. Ray moved the ice back, then took his screwdriver and removed a piece of the floor. He put the package in the compartment, put the floor back in place, and covered it with ice and shrimp. He made several trips between the boat and truck, moving all the shrimp from one to the other. Finally the truck was loaded. He drove off the pier and headed to Wilmington. He drove around back of W & W seafood. The roll up door was already open, so he pulled in, and backed the truck up to a large bin full of ice. Then he got out and waited beside the truck.

Amos Black approached him grinning, "well Ray you have a good catch" said Black.

"Yeah, I've got a nice load of shrimp. The special cargo's right where it's supposes to be."

"Good, you go up to the office while I get the seafood unloaded and weighted, then I'll come up and pay you."

Once the truck was empty Black always checked the package before he paid up. He was the type of guy that didn't trust anyone. As long as they had been in business together he should have known the brothers wouldn't screw him, but he always checked behind them. Ray waited in the office for twenty minutes before Black came in.

"You did real well Ray," said Black "I'll write you a check for the shrimp."

Black wrote a check and handed it to Ray. Then he opened his desk drawer, took out a plain manila envelope, and gave it to him.

“Thanks” said Ray “I should have some more seafood later this month, of course you know it’ll be two months before the next special load is due. That’ll be about the end of fishing season. Remember what we talked about last time. Joe and I are going to take our girlfriends, move away, and start over.”

“Everything’s going so good,” answered Black “I think we could go on for a long time, but if you guys are determined to leave what can I do. You could make a lot of money if you just stayed in the business a few more years.”

“It’s been a good deal for all of us, but it’s time to get out. We haven't even got to enjoy any of our money yet. Joe only gets to see his girl every two months, and I‘ve had enough of working my tail off on the boat. We‘re both ready for a change. If we stay here we’ll always have to worry about the law catching up with us. I don‘t know about Joe, but I’m soon going to give my girl a ring.

Ray left the office and got into his own truck, which he had left at W & W Seafood when he had picked up the refrigerated truck. He opened the envelope; inside was a neat stack of one hundred dollar bills. Black had never tried to cheat on their deal, so he was sure the total would be twenty thousand dollars. He opened the glove compartment and put the envelope inside it. Then he drove by the bank and cashed the check. Next he headed to the state port to pick up Joe. He knew that eventually the dope would be on its way to feed all the addicts in our nation’s capitol. W & W stood for Wilmington and Washington.

CHAPTER 4

When Ray got to the state port, Joe was nowhere in sight. He was usually waiting beside the guardhouse. The guard told Ray that the Coast Guard and DEA were doing a surprise drug search on the Emerald Thai. Nobody was allowed to leave until they were finished. Ray drove into the parking lot and parked. He just sat in his truck and listened to the radio. Half and hour later Joe walked out to the truck. He threw his bags in the back and climbed in the passenger side.

“Damn the Coast Guard and DEA,” he gripped “I had to wait until those guys checked every nook and cranny of the ship. As many times as they’ve checked us they ought to know they won’t find any drugs. They always try to surprise us, but they never find anything. It’d blow their minds if they knew what was going on right under their noses. Did everything go all right with the pick up?”

“Everything went fine,” answered Ray “the moneys in the glove compartment.”

“Did you tell Black we’re only going to bring in one more load?”

“Yeah, he’s pretty pissed off about it. I’m sure he would like to keep operating for a few more years, but like I told him, it’s time for us to get out and enjoy our money. Maybe he can find somebody else to bring the stuff in for him.”

“Damn right it’s time for us to start spending some of our money. I’ve told the captain the next trip will be my last. I’ve had it with spending all my life on a ship. Let’s take our money, and girls, and get the hell out of Oak Island. We’ll move someplace new where we can enjoy life. You know we’re not getting any younger. I want to wake up with a warm body next to me for the rest of my life. If Black wants to keep bringing in dope that‘s his problem. If he keeps bringing the stuff in he’ll eventually get caught. When that happens we want to make sure there’s no way he can find us. He knows we‘ll never tell anybody he deals in dope. That‘s all he should be worried about. We‘re just as guilty as he is, but now it‘s time for us to get out.”

“Black lives pretty good up in Wilmington,” replied Ray “everybody thinks he makes all his money from his seafood warehouses. He can spend as much money as he wants to without anyone questioning him. You and I have to live the same way we always have and work like we did before we got any money. After all the risk we’ve took bringing dope in, he ought to realize it’s time for us to live pretty good to.”

“He ought to but he’s just a greedy bastard. After the next trip Black can go to hell as far as I’m concerned. I don’t ever want to see the son of a bitch again. Let’s not worry about him this week. I just want to enjoy my time at home.

“Good idea, let’s forget our problems for one week and have some fun. I know the girls are ready for some partying.”

The guys were in a very good mood as they traveled toward home. They had been bringing in dope for over two years and now the end was in sight. Now they were dreaming of a bright future, and they had found the ones they wanted to share it with.

"It's good to be home," said Joe as he entered the house "I feel like I've been on the ocean for ten years. Call the girls and make a date for tonight. I'm going to take a nap. Wake me up around five o'clock."

The guy's girlfriends shared an apartment in the nearby town of Shallotte. Carol, Ray's girl, and Mona, Joe's girl, both worked at the American Chemical plant in Wilmington. They both hated their jobs but the money was good. Ray knew the girls would be at work, so he left a message on their answering machine to meet at their favorite bar at eight that night. The girls knew Joe was coming home today, so they were expecting to get together that night. It was Friday, so Carol and Mona could spend the night with them. It was time to hide the money. In the back of the house was a small den that contained a large fireplace. The fireplace could actually heat the whole house, but the brothers hadn't used it since their father's death. However they did leave ashes and some wood in the fireplace. It always looked as if it was used regularly. Ray removed the wood and raked the ashes to the side. The hearth was made of several flat stones. The middle stone was much larger than the others were. Ray worked the poker under the front of the middle stone and raised it up. He moved the stone to the side; under it was a compartment containing a small safe. Ray took out the safe and opened it. Inside it were several rows, piled high with one hundred dollar bills. He took the money out of the envelope and put it on top of the bills. He knew exactly how much money was in the safe without counting it. I guess now's a good time to quite the business he thought, the safe's about full. He put the safe back, replaced the stone, and covered it with ashes and wood. No one would ever question why two guys living together kept such a messy house. He went out to the boat and worked on his nets for a few hours. Then he woke up Joe.

The most popular bar on the island is called the Sea Hut. The guys walked in at exactly eight o'clock. Carol and Mona were already sitting at a table. Mona ran to Joe and gave him a big hug.

"God! I thought you would never get home," She said.

"Yeah, I know, these trips at sea are getting to be old. Guess what! I'm only going to make one more. I told the captain the next trip would be my last. After that I'm all yours baby. I'm not spending all my life on a ship. I'm going to stay here with you and enjoy the rest of my life."

Mona almost shouted back, "you're not kidding me are you. You're really going to quit?"

"You got it baby," replied Joe "I've got to make one more trip to settle some things out then I'm finished. You think you can get used to having me around?

Mona was almost speechless, she finally shouted out, "I love having you around and you know it."

While the two of them were celebrating, Ray walked over and kissed Carol on the cheek.

"It's sure good to see you babe," he said

"You too," she answered "I've been thinking about you all day."

Mona finally released her grip on Joe enough for them to walk over to the table. They all sat down and ordered a round of beers.

"Joe if you quit your job what will you do?" asked Mona.

"Don't worry about a thing," answered Joe "all the time I've been at sea I didn't need to spend much money. I've got a nice nest egg built up. I'll help Ray on the boat for a while then we'll see what happens. I've got a good education, so I'm not worried about finding a job."

He leaned over, gave her a kiss, and whispered in her ear "some things are more important than money."

"I sure can use some help on the boat," replied Ray "when I get a net full of shrimp it's about more then one man can handle. I can't afford to hire anyone full time though. Besides it'll be nice to have somebody to talk to out there."

Neither of the brothers wanted to tell the girls what they were really planning to do. They would surprise them after they brought the last load of dope in.

The four of them had a good time at the bar. Drinking beer, playing pool, shooting the breeze, and dancing to the music from the jukebox. They all danced when the slow songs were playing, and drank beer while the fast ones played. Several times Joe and Mona kept dancing after the music had stopped. Ray and Carol had a good laugh watching them. Around eleven o'clock Ray whispered to Carol, "I don't blame Joe for not staying on with the ship. No job is worth being away from the woman you love."

Carol grabbed his hand and gave it a squeeze. She didn't need to talk; the look in her eyes was all the answer Ray needed. It was time to leave the bar. He certainly didn't have a problem getting Joe and Mona to leave; they were more than ready to be alone. They went to the brother's house, watched a little TV, and drank a few more beers. At midnight Joe grabbed Mona's hand and said,

"It's been fun, but I've been gone a long time, it's time for us to hit the hay."

They went into Joe's bedroom. Ray went into his own bedroom while Carol changed clothes in the bathroom. Ray waited patiently in the bed for Carol. She soon appeared in the doorway wearing a nightie that left nothing to the imagination. She slid under the sheet and curled up next to him. Ray gave her a warm kiss and held her tight. He thought back to the first time he had saw her. It was about a year ago. He and Joe were at the Oak Island public beach access. Carol and Mona lay on a blanket about twenty feet in front of them. She was so beautiful he couldn't keep his eyes off her. She had long jet-black hair, a great figure, and the most beautiful smile he'd ever seen. From the moment he first saw her he wanted to kiss those great looking lips. Joe had to admit he wouldn't mind meeting her friend. Joe bet him ten dollars that he wouldn't go talk to her, but Ray was much to shy for that. However, he did think of a plan to meet her. When Carol went into the water, he went out beyond her. It was no accident when he bodysurfed into her legs, knocking her down. Ray apologized but she thought it was funny. They started talking, and Carol invited the brothers over. Joe and Mona hit it off as well, and the four of them had been together ever since. Mona resembles Carol so much they are often mistaken for sisters.

The girls were originally from Charlotte. They were both twenty-six, and had been best friends from the first grade all the way through high school. After graduating they decided to live their dream and moved to the beach. They moved to Myrtle Beach and shared an apartment. The only jobs they could find were waiting tables at a local restaurant. Their rent took most of their money, and it soon became tough to make ends meet. When they heard the American Chemical plant in Wilmington was hiring they both got jobs there. They found an apartment in Shallotte so they could be close to work and the beach.

Carol was different from any woman Ray had been with. When they made love there was a passion, and tenderness he had never known before. Sometimes he had the feeling that they were meant to be together. I'm head over heels in love with her he thought. Someday soon I'll marry her and take her away from this place. As soon as the last coke shipment was through he was planning to give her a ring.

Since the brothers met the girls Ray had actually felt sorry for Joe and Mona. He got to see Carol every weekend, while Joe was stuck at sea, and only got to see Mona every two months. He would go over to the girl's apartment Friday thru Sunday nights. Most weekends they didn't do anything special, just hang out, and watch TV, or go to a movie. They were happy just being together. They didn't want Mona to feel left out so they tried to include her in the fun. She had to get lonely while Joe was gone, but she never complained. Joe had made a lot of changes in his life during the past year. He used to come home bragging about his antics with the Thai whores. Now he comes home complaining about how long the trip was. No more stories about the good times. He was faithful to Mona and wasn't happy being separated from her. He knew it was time to decide between his job and his girl. The job would have to go.

When Joe came home everything changed. They would all be together the whole week. The girls would spend the weekend with the brothers or vice versa. Sometimes they would go down to Myrtle Beach, and enjoy the carnival rides, or go to a nightclub. Sometimes they would just go to the Sea Hut, enjoy a few beers, and just hang out. Sometimes each couple would just enjoy a little quiet time by themselves. Sometimes Joe would go out on the boat with him, and sometimes he wouldn't even fish the whole week. It would always be a great week, but it always went by to fast. He didn't blame Joe for wanting to stay at home. He would give up any job in the world if it kept him and Carol apart. Now thanks to the money they had made in the drug business, they could give up their jobs, take the girls, and move away. They wouldn't be rich, but they had enough to start life new some place else. They knew it was time to get out now; greed is what usually gets people caught. If Amos Black wanted to keep bringing dope in, he could find somebody else to help him. Once they moved away from Oak Island they would never see Black again. They weren't about to tell him where they were moving to.

He was startled from his dreaming by Carol's voice, "you seem like you're far away," she said "what are you thinking about?"

Ray gave her a long kiss. Then he answered; "I'm just thinking about how much I love you and how wonderful this is. I could lay here in your arms forever."

Carol flashed that beautiful smile at him and said, "I love you to."

Then she gave him a big kiss.

He was tempted to ask her to marry him right away. I'll have to fight temptation he thought. When we get married everything will be perfect, and it can't be perfect as long as I'm in the dope business. I'll only have to wait two more months. Then we can have a short engagement and get married as soon as possible. Two months will go by fast.

CHAPTER 5

Ray woke early in the morning with Carol's head on his shoulder. Something was making an awful noise in his head. I didn't drink that much last night he thought. He finally realized that the noise wasn't his head ringing, but the telephone beside his bed. Still half asleep he picked up the receiver and mumbled, "Hello."

"Wake up pretty boy," said Amos Black.

"Black what the hell are you doing calling here this early in the morning," answered Ray.

"I've got a job for you and Joe. One of our drivers had an accident. I need you guys to drive a load up to Washington. I'll pay you a cool grand apiece. Just drive one truck up there, then turn around, and drive another one back. It'll be the easiest thousand bucks you ever made. You know I can't trust just any driver with the merchandise in that truck."

Ray thought a second then answered, "When do you want us to leave?"

"Be at my office at nine o'clock."

Ray replied, “I’ll wake Joe and ask him, if he don’t want to go I’ll call you back, if I don’t call we’ll be there at nine. I don‘t see how we can turn down a thousand bucks each just to drive to D.C.”

“I’m sure you won’t turn it down,” said Black “I’ll be looking for you at nine.” Ray hung up the phone and woke Carol up.

“The guy I sell shrimp to in Wilmington needs me and Joe to drive a load of seafood to Washington,” he said, “his regular driver was in an accident. He’s going to pay us very well to do it. I’m going to wake up Joe and see if he wants to go. If we go, it’ll be early in the morning before we get back.”

He didn’t want to tell her exactly how much money he’d get. She might question why anyone would pay a thousand bucks just to drive to Washington. Ray got up and knocked on Joe’s door. He explained what Black wanted them to do and told him how much money they would make. Joe was still reluctant to go,

this was his time off, and he wanted to spend the whole day with Mona. He woke Mona up and asked her what she would like for him to do. She said he couldn’t turn down good money just to drive to Washington, besides she would be here when he got back. They would be together the rests of the week.

“OK” said Joe, “I’m only going because the money’s so good. This is sure not how I wanted to spend my Saturday when I’m at home. Let’s go get it over with. I want to get back as soon as we can.”

“We’ll just drive up there then turn around and come straight back,” replied Ray “we’ll still spend tomorrow with the girls.”

They told the girls to sleep as long as they wanted to, and they would call them the next day. Then they headed for Black's office. They walked in at exactly nine o'clock.

"Good morning," said Black "sorry to get you guys up so early, but we've got to get this load to Washington today. Our regular driver was in an accident yesterday, and nobody else knows about the special cargo in the truck. I trust you guys to get the stuff up there. Just be careful and obey the traffic laws, we don't want the cops stopping the truck for any reason. The back door is locked, and you won't have a key to open it."

He handed Ray a slip of paper with a phone number on it, "call this number when you get there, and they'll tell you what to do. Take exit 32, just as you get in the city, there's a big shopping center there. You can use the pay phone there. Don't use your cell phone, you never can tell who might listen in."

Then he handed Ray a single key; "they'll pay you when you get up there. It'll be early in the morning before you get back, just park the truck in front of the roll up door, and drop the key in the box next to it."

He then showed them the truck they would drive. It looked like the same truck Ray had driven up the day before. A solid white truck with no markings on it. Ray knew the dope was still hid in the secret compartment. He's probably got everything fixed, so if anything goes wrong, it can't be traced back to him he thought. When it came to business Black was sharp as a tack.

"Ok" said Ray "we just drive up there then turn around and drive right back."

"That's all you gotta do," answered Black "the people up there will show you where to take this truck, and give you another one to drive back. You guys have a nice trip, and be sure you drive safely, remember we can't have the cops checking this truck for any reason."

Ray got in the drivers seat and Joe got in the passenger seat. Ray cranked up the truck and drove out of the building. They drove out of the city, up interstate 40, to interstate 95, and on toward Washington.

"So we're finally going to see where the dope ends up at," said Joe

"Yeah" answered Ray "we always knew it went to Washington, it'll be interesting to see what kind of operation Black has up there. I always wondered how many people were involved in the scheme."

"You don't think he could be setting us up for something do you? You know he's pretty pissed off at us. He's not ready to get out of the dope business."

"I'm not worried about that," replied Ray "Black's a good businessman. He just wants to get the dope up to Washington. That's where all the moneys made. This'll just be a one time thing for us. I'm sure by the next shipment his driver will be mended up or he'll have a new one. We're just helping him out of a bind, besides look at all the money he's paying us."

"Yeah the money's great. There's still something about that guy I don't trust though."

"I have to admit, I'll be glad when we're through dealing with him," answered Ray "those shifty eyes of his give me the creeps. Plus he's so fat he walks like a penguin."

They stopped one time in Richmond for gas and a bite to eat. Joe drove from there on to Washington. It was just starting to get dark when they arrived in the city. They took exit

32, pulled in the shopping center, and called the phone number. They were told to just wait where they were and someone would come for them. They waited for at least an hour before a blue SUV pulled up next to them. A bald headed man about fifty years old stuck his head out the window and said,

"You must be the guys from Carolina"

"That's right," nodded Joe

My name's Pete, just follow me," was the answer "You guys stay close because this place is hard to find, and you sure don't want to get lost in this city."

It was pitch dark when they left the shopping center. They followed Pete several miles deep into the city. Up and down streets, in and out of housing projects, it seemed like they would never get to Black's place. One thing for sure, the brothers were totally lost, they could never find this place again. They finally drove around back of an old warehouse, and through an open door. The building resembled the one back in Wilmington. Neither of them would win a prize for beauty. There were large bins along one wall just like the ones at the warehouse in Wilmington. Pete had them back the truck up to a bin beside one that had fertilizer wrote on it. These guys think of everything thought Ray, fish heads, and guts make great fertilizer.

After they parked the truck Ray ask Pete, "what do you do with the bin marked fertilizer?"

"We take that to a fertilizer plant about twenty miles north of here," replied Pete "everything is dumped into a giant bin up there, and then ground up into fertilizer. The place stinks like hell. As soon as we're finished here my driver will haul it up there. You guys go wait in the office while we unload the truck. Then I'll come up and pay you. There's some cold beer in the fridge if you want one."

The brothers went to the office, got a beer, and made themselves comfortable. Half an hour later Pete came in the door.

"You guys did good," he said "everything's right where it's suppose to be. We don't mind paying good money for good service."

He handed Ray an envelope with twenty one hundred dollar bills in it.

Then he handed him a key and said, "you'll drive the truck in front of yours back to Wilmington. Before you guys leave there's something I want to show you."

The brothers were definitely interested in seeing more of Black's operation in D.C.

They followed Pete back into the warehouse. The place was empty except for a muscular black man standing beside the truck they had just driven in. That must be the driver going to the fertilizer plant thought Ray. Pete went to the back of the truck and opened the door. The ice had been pushed to the side to reveal a gray tarp under it. Pete pulled back the tarp and there laid the frozen body of a man.

"Take a good look," said Pete

The brothers didn't have to be told. They both stood there with their mouths half open.

"This ass hole used to work for us," said Pete "he got greedy, tried to keep some of our money, now he's going to be fertilizer. Nobody pulls anything on us," he growled "nobody! We own you punks, you do what we say when we say it, or you'll be fertilizer to. Who the hell do you two punks think you are? You think just because you're tired of bringing stuff in you can just decide to quit. You don't get out of this business until we're through with you. It'll be a long time before we're ready to stop. I don't see what the hell you two are complaining about anyway; ol Black pays you good money. In case one of you don't mind being plant food, remember this, Black knows all about your little girlfriends back home. It would be a shame to mess those pretty face's up. And don't get the idea you can run off, and hide somewhere, or go to the cops. You'll just piss ol' Black off more. There's nowhere you can go that he won't find you and your little girlfriends. If you think the cops can protect you you're crazy as hell. You two idiots have no idea what a son of a bitch Black can be. He'd think no more about killing you then he did this ass hole in the truck. I guarantee you one thing, if the cops ever get Black he'll be out on bail in no time. Then he'll come after your little girlfriends first thing. He might even fix it so he can kill all four of you at the same time. Now get your butts in that truck, and get back to Carolina. Just keep driving south, eventually you'll get out of the city."

The brothers were both so stunned they couldn't say anything. Ray got behind the wheel and Joe got in the passenger side of the truck. They drove out of the warehouse and headed south. It seemed like they drove twenty miles before they found the interstate. Neither man said a word as they drove down the highway. They couldn't talk; they were horrified at what they had just seen, and by what Pete had told them.

After half an hour of silence Ray said, "Joe what the hell have we got ourselves into. All we wanted to do was made a little extra money. I never dreamed anybody would get killed."

"Me neither," replied Joe "I never thought Black would resort to murder to keep us in the dope business. I wonder who that guy was? Have you ever seen him before?"

“I’ve never seen him before,” answered Ray “but Pete made it clear that Black had killed him. He must have been in the back of the truck the whole trip up here. They’re going to grind him up and make fertilizer out of him. What kind of people are we dealing with? How could anybody do that to another human being? The worst thing is Black knows about our girls. How are we ever going to get out of this mess?

“I don’t know,” said Joe “we’ve got a lot of thinking to do, I’ll tell you one thing though, nobody owns me.”

“But what can we do? I believe what Pete told us. There’s nowhere we can go to get away from Black, and we sure can’t put the girls in danger. But if that fat, pig faced, son of a bitch, lays a finger on those girls, I’ll cut his throat, and gladly watch his life drain out of his body like the pig he is.”

“You‘ll have to get to him before I do,” replied Joe “the most important thing is we’ve got to make sure he never gets the chance to hurt the girls. I’ve told the captain I would only make one more trip and that’s all I’m planning to make. I’m sure he would let me stay on, but I don’t want to. I’m going to take Mona and get the hell out of Oak Island, and Amos Black is not going to stop me. I’m sure you want to do the same thing with Carol, so we’ve got to think of something.”

The rest of the trip was mostly silent. Both brothers were deep in thought. They just wanted to hurry up and get home. They were still pretty shaken by what happened in D.C. They stopped once for gas and coffee, and made good time getting to Wilmington. They pulled into the W & W parking lot around five AM, parked the truck in front of the roll up door, and put the key in the box. Then they got in Ray’s truck and headed for Oak Island. When they got home they both tried to get some sleep but it was useless. Their minds kept repeating seeing the frozen body in the truck, and the chilling warning that Pete had gave them. Finally around noon they just gave up on sleep and called the girls. Maybe they could still enjoy the weekend a little.

It was a beautiful day, and the girls wanted to go to the beach. They packed a cooler with drinks and sandwiches, and went to the public beach access. Laying on a blanket with the girls next to them the guys should have had a great time. They put on a good face, but all either of them could think of was the events of the day before. The girls were as happy as larks. They had on idea their lives could be in danger. All they knew was Joe was home; they would have fun for a week. Just watching the girls laugh made the brothers feel very protective of them. Amos Black was never going to hurt their girls or keep them from being together. No matter what they had to do, they would stop him.

When they returned home from the beach Ray noticed there was a message on their answering machine. He waited until the girls left then he played it. It was Amos Black telling them to call him at a certain number. Ray dialed the number and recognized Black's voice when he said hello.

"Black, you son of a bitch, you knew what was in that truck all the time," he said with anger in his voice.

"Well, like I told you, one of our drivers had an accident," answered Black "I hope you guys got the message, you do what we say, when we say it, or you'll have an accident too. We got a good thing going here, and I don't want to hear any more talk about stopping. We're all making to much money to end things now. By the way, I know exactly where your little girlfriends live. I've followed you over there several times. Tell

Joe he'll keep bringing the stuff in like always, or his girl won't be here when he gets back. She'll be out fertilizing a field somewhere, along with yours."

Then he slammed the phone down.

Ray turned to Joe and said, "that son of a bitch said he'd followed us over to the girl's place. He said he knew exactly where they live. He also said you'd have to keep bringing the dope in, or he'd make fertilizer out of both of them. After what we saw in D.C. I'm sure he'd do it."

"We've got to think of something fast," replied Joe "Black don't think we've got balls enough to do anything to him. He thinks he can just boss us around and we'll set back and take it. Well he's got another think coming. He wants to play rough, so we'll have to play rough to. We'll have to come up with a plan that gets us out of the dope business, and takes care of Black at the same time."

They both got a beer and sat at the kitchen table in silence.

Finally Joe said, "have you ever dealt with anyone at W & W Seafood beside Amos Black?"

"No" answered Ray "Black's the only one. I don't even know anybody else there."

"How about the people in Washington, do you think Pete knows our names and where we live?"

"I doubt it; he never did call us by name. It's not the kind of thing you keep records on. I think Pete was just saying what Black told him to say."

Joe stood up and put his foot on his chair, then said, "so if Amos Black were out of the way nobody would know about us and the dope."

The room was so silent you could have heard a pin drop. Finally Ray picked up his beer and finished drinking it. Then he said

"You're thinking we could kill Black, is that it. I'll have to admit I've thought about it to, especially after what he said about the girls, but I don't know if I could really do it."

"If that's the only way we can get out of this mess, that's what we'll have to do. I read in a book once that under the right circumstances anybody could commit murder," replied Joe "just think of it as killing a wild pig, a great big pig. That's about all he is anyway. We've got to think about the rest of our lives. We can't have a normal life as long as Blacks around. If we get rid of him, and move away from this place, we can live the way we deserve to."

"But Joe do you really think you could kill somebody, even somebody as disgusting as Black?"

"As pissed off as I am right now, hell yes, I could kill Black. He wouldn't think twice about killing us and the girls."

"And what if we get caught, then instead of dealing in dope we'll have a first degree murder charge against us. They could put us to death for that, or we could spend the rest of our lives in prison."

"You want to think about Carol being ground up and made into fertilizer? You and I can take care of ourselves, but we've got to get that bastard to protect the girls. We've got to figure out a way to do it and never get caught. We've got two months before the next shipment is due. We'll both be thinking of different ways to do it during that time. Between the two of us I'm sure we can come up with a plan that will work.

One thing for sure, this will be my last trip to sea, and I'll have plenty of time to think. When I get back Amos Black will have to go."

"Ok, we'll come up with something, but let's think about Black after you leave. I'm sick of this whole mess. In the mean time let's try to enjoy the rest of your time at home."

"That's exactly what I plan to do," replied Joe "I'm going to see Mona every day I'm at home. Black's not going to ruin the little time I get to spend with her. I'll worry about him when I'm back on the ship."

The brothers were able to put Black in the back of their minds for the rest of the week. They were able to see the girls every night and really enjoy themselves. Like every week Joe was at home it went by way to fast. Sunday afternoon arrived, and it was time for Joe to ship out. He left Mona crying at her apartment, and Ray drove him to the State Port.

"Remember," said Joe "we've got to think of a way to do Black in. I'm not leaving Mona again. I don't care what I have to do. I'll make this last trip for Black, and then I'm finished. If I have to kill the son of a bitch to get out I'm willing to do it."

"Maybe he'll change his mind while you're gone, but I doubt it. We've got enough time for at least one of us to come up with a good plan," replied Ray "that's probably all I'll think about while I'm out on the Carolina. With all the time you have on the ship you could drive yourself crazy thinking about Black."

"He's not going to drive me crazy," replied Joe "I'll just work out twice as much as I usually do. I'll keep the stress worked off. You can bet money on one thing though; Black will be on my mind the whole trip."

CHAPTER 6

Ray left Joe at the state port and returned to the girl's apartment. He was feeling very protective of both girls. Joe would be gone for two months. It was up to him to make sure the girls were safe. Even though this drug trip should go the way all the others had, he just didn't trust Amos Black. If Black got the idea the brothers were determined to get out of the business, there was no telling what he would do. Ray knew he would have to be careful; he didn't want the girls to know anything was wrong. He stayed at the apartment until eleven o'clock then he went home. This was his usual routine on the day Joe left. He told Carol he would call her the next day and promised to do something special the next weekend.

Ray quickly settled back into his routine of working on the boat all week and seeing Carol on weekends. No one noticed the fact that he went to the girl's place a little earlier than usual and stayed a little later. He acted so normal not even Carol could tell anything was wrong. Just as he had predicted he worried about Black every time he went out in the boat. Weekends with Carol were his only relief from the constant worrying. Only God knew what would happen when the last drug trip was over. Time seemed to drag by but eventually two months pasted. Joe would soon be home and the brother's lives would change forever.

It was the day before the Emerald Thai was due at the two-mile buoy. Ray had caught a nice load of shrimp and had sold them at the local wholesale warehouse. He hadn't seen or talked to Black since the phone call after the D.C. trip. He was thinking, maybe I have to deal dope with Black, but I sure as hell don't have to sell my seafood to him. Ray had just tied off the Carolina when his cell phone rang.

"Hello" he said

"Well Ray, where you been keeping yourself," answered Amos Black "I haven't saw you in a long time. There's no reason we can't be friends. I just wanted to remind you that Joe's ship is due in tomorrow."

"Black is there anything you don't know," replied Ray

"Oh there's a few things I don't know, but I do know the schedule of the Emerald Thai," said Black "I also know that Joe received the package in Thailand just like he was supposed to. I just wanted to make sure you guys realize what will happen if I don't get that package."

"Don't worry," answered Ray "I'll be there in about an hour to pick up the truck. Everything will go the same way it always has."

"Good" replied Black "I'll see you in about an hour, and everything had better go like its suppose to."

Ray hated the very idea of seeing Black. During the past two months he had thought of a dozen ways to kill him and get rid of his body. He also thought of a dozen reasons why his ideas wouldn't work. There was nothing he could think of that didn't end with him and Joe getting caught by the police. He was tired of thinking about the whole mess. Joe was the smart one. Joe would come up with a good plan and they'd make sure it worked. Ray went in the house and washed up. Then he got in his truck and headed for Wilmington.

Ray parked his truck in the W & W parking lot and walked in the buildings side door. Black had already checked out the refrigerated truck and parked it next to the roll up door. The two men met beside the truck.

"It's good to see you Ray," said Black

"Cut out the small talk," answered Ray "I just want to pick up the truck and get out of here. I might have to do business with you Black, but I sure as hell don't have to like you."

"I don't give a damn if you like me or not. Just make sure you get my package to me. The key is in the truck, take it and get the hell out of here."

Ray got in the truck and drove out of the building. He got on the highway and headed for Oak Island. The next few days could be very interesting he thought.

One good thing about being your own boss, if you don't want to work one day you don't have to. Ray woke up early the next morning and decided he wouldn't fish that day. Even though it was early October, and the fishing was good, he was just too nervous. He would work around the house and on the boat while he waited for Joe to call. Joe had told him he didn't want to say too much over the ship's phone. You never know who might be listening in on a ship to shore call. The Coast Guard and the DEA had very sophisticated eavesdropping equipment. It was just another weapon in the war against dope smuggling. That's why they always referred to the package as the special cargo. Joe said if he had a plan that they could work on right away he would only give bits and pieces of it over the ship's phone. If Ray didn't understand everything, he would tell Joe his phone was breaking up, and to call back when he got to port. It was two o'clock when Ray's cell phone rang.

"Hello" he said

"It's me Ray," answered Joe "we're at the two mile buoy. We should be at the state port at one tomorrow. It's been a good trip; everything has gone exactly like it was suppose to. I want to celebrate my last trip tomorrow night. I've already called the Southside Motel and booked a room. I'll be in room number seventeen. It's the last bottom room on the backside. That way we can get stinking drunk and won't have to drive. The motel is on the way to the place where you sell your shrimp. Stop by there and pick me up on your way in. Bring along a change of cloths for each of us, we don't want to smell like beer the next day. After you unload your shrimp we'll start hitting the bars. Don't come too early though: maybe six o'clock. I'll take a nap until then. You can always make up an excuse for getting to the seafood place late. I'm going to call Mona and tell her the crew is giving me a party tomorrow night and you're coming to. That way it'll be just the two of us, just like the old days. We'll see the girls the day after tomorrow. By the way I want you to bring my bow and quiver of arrows. Deer seasons in now, and I'll have plenty of time to hunt. We'll go to that indoor range and shoot a little. Make sure you bring our boots to. We want our practice to be as realistic as possible. Do you understand everything I need?"

"Yeah" answered Ray "I understand everything. I'll see you tomorrow evening."

Ray backed the refrigerated truck as far on the pier as he could. Then he started shoveling ice from the truck to the boat's hole. He kept shoveling until the bottom of the hole was completely covered with ice. He would still have to catch some shrimp the next day and he had to keep them fresh. When he had everything ready for the next morning he went in the house and took a long shower. He drank a couple of beers to try to calm his nerves. Joe hadn't explained exactly what his plan was but he was sure of one thing: tomorrow they were going to kill a man. No matter what Black had done, or threatened to do, could they justify taking his life? When the time came could they really do it? How would they do it, and what would they do with his body? Would it be something that would haunt them for the rest of their lives? Finally what if they got caught, all their plans for a new life with the girls would be shot to hell. Damn you Black he thought, why didn't you just let us out of the mess? Why did you force us to become murders? It's not something we want to do, but you brought it on yourself. A few months ago he would have laughed if someone had suggested he and Joe could kill anybody, now he was worried sick knowing they actually would. When he had picked up the refrigerated truck Black acted like he normally did. He had no idea what the guys were planning to do to him. He probably thought they didn't have guts enough to do anything. He had made one big mistake; he had threatened to harm their girlfriends. Just the fact that Black knew where the girls lived made Ray's stomach tighten up. No doubt about it, they had to get rid of Black. He wondered if Joe was as agonized as he was. Joe was the kind of guy who would never act unless he was sure everything would work out right. Whatever they did, Joe would have planned right down to the smallest detail. Still even the best made plans can go wrong. Ray wished the time would go by faster. This was the worst part, having to wait and think. He was feeling very lonely. He thought about calling Carol but decided not to. By now Joe should have called Mona and told her they would be over the day after tomorrow. There was nothing he could add to that. He drank a few more beers and tried to watch television. It was hopeless; his mind kept going over all the different things that could happen. At ten o'clock he went to bed. He had already thought of a good excuse for getting to Wilmington late the next day. What he needed now was at least a few hours of sleep.

The alarm clock was buzzing at three am. Ray got up and washed his face with cold water. He made a pot of coffee and a bowl of cereal. Sitting at the kitchen table he felt totally exhausted. He hadn't slept worth a darn. He kept thinking about a crazy dream he had. He dreamed he was fishing near the two-mile buoy. His net hadn't been in the water long, but it seemed like it was full. He started reeling his net in, but he didn't see any fish. His net was half way in, but he still didn't see any fish. Something very heavy was still in the net. He brought the last of the net in the boat, and there wrapped up in the net was Amos Black's body. He woke up with sweat dripping off his forehead.

Ray poured the coffee into a thermos and walked out to the Carolina. It was a very dark night; he would definitely have to use his spotlight just to find his way to the two-mile buoy. He eased the boat down the canal, into the waterway and on out to sea. Just after he crossed the breakers he saw what looked like lights sitting on the ocean. He knew it was the Emerald Thai. Ten minutes later he was dropping anchor at the two-mile buoy. Shinning his spotlight over the ocean surface he finally saw the image of white. He took his gaff and pulled the image into the boat. Just like always there was the package containing five kilos of coke. He carried the package down into the boats hole and hid it in the secret compartment. After covering the package with ice he moved the Carolina about a mile from the ship. Then he poured a cup of coffee and waited for daylight. This was one of the few times he noticed how beautiful the island was at night. The island's lights seemed to twinkle like stars. Before long orange streaks of light appeared on the horizon. Ray wondered how many people ever get to see a beautiful sunrise. It was a perfect time, watching the daylight replace the darkness. It would be great if time could stand still and he could stay in this beautiful place forever. Of course he would have to have Carol with him. He wished that warm fuzzy feeling could last a lot longer but it was time for him to get busy. It was very important to hurry up and get some shrimp on top of the ice. He lowered his nets and began trawling parallel to the shore. He trawled for about two hours then brought his nets it. There was just enough shrimp to cover the top of the ice in the boat's hole. That was all he wanted on this trip. Ray turned on the radio, poured some more coffee, and sat back in his chair. He would be in no hurry today. To make the time go by he tried to think about all the trips he had taken with his father.

Every time he thought about fishing with his dad one particular trip always came to mind. He and his dad were trawling about three miles from shore. It was a cloudy and windy day. They were both concentrating on the nets when they suddenly noticed a heavy fog had moved in. In a matter of seconds it was so foggy they couldn't see for more than a few feet. Of course they had a radio and compass but in this situation they weren't much help. They could only tell what direction they were traveling in not if they were about to hit anything. His dad calmly stopped the Carolina and dropped the anchor. Then he pulled the nets in. By the time they had all the fish and shrimp in the boat's hole the fog had lifted enough for them to see the shore. They decided not to tempt fate and made a beeline for land while they could see the way.

His next most memorable trip happened when he was ten years old. Ray, Joe, and their dad were planning to fish at least for half a day. Ray had eaten a bunch of pancakes for breakfast before they left home. It was a very hot day in July. By the time they got the nets in the water Ray was feeling sick. He leaned over the side of the boat and threw up until he thought his guts were coming out. Nobody ever forgets the first time they got seasick. Neither Joe nor his dad laughed at him. In fact his dad did a very unusual thing. He pulled the nets in and they went back home. Oh, how wonderful it was to get back on dry land. Ray would never forget the compassion his father showed that day. How many seasick passengers have prayed for their boat to get back to shore? Ray felt better the next morning but he had no desire to go back out on the boat. His father calmly told him the only way to overcome fear was to face it head on. Ray went back out that day. He has never been seasick again.

There had been to many trips to remember them all. Most of them had been good trips, but a few were not so good. Some days they would have the nets out all day and barely catch anything. Other days the nets would be so full of fish and shrimp they could hardly pull them in. Ray had worked with his dad as far back as he could remember. Right up until the time his dad was too weak to go out on the boat. The two of them had formed a great friendship and respect for each other. His dad always knew the right thing to do. How he wished his dad were here now. He'd know the best way for the brothers to get out of the mess they were in. Just thinking about him helped a lot. Ray had to keep his mind occupied or he would worry himself sick. He just couldn't bear to think about what would happen later that day. At noon he could see the Emerald Thai heading for the state port. Everything was right on schedule. An hour later he dialed Amos Black on his cell phone.

"Hello" answered Black

"Black it's me," replied Ray "I'm running late. Damn fuel pump went out on my boat. I've been working on it for the past two hours. I can't get the engine running. I'm waiting for a towboat to pull me in."

"Son of a bitch," answered Black "I've got to have that shipment here today. How long is it going to take?"

"Don't know," said Ray "like I said, I'm waiting for the towboat now. I'll call you when I get to shore."

"You damn sure better," said Black "why the hell didn't you call the towboat sooner?

"I thought I could get it fixed," replied Ray "I've got a box full of tools with me. The pump's shot, it's going to have to be replaced."

"Just hurry the hell up," answered Black.

Ray went back to his coffee and radio; he was just killing time. For some reason he was more relaxed then he had been the day before. Maybe thinking about his father had calmed his nerves. Maybe it was because he knew everything would soon be over. Finally at four o'clock he headed for home. As soon as he docked the boat he called Amos Black.

"Black" he said, "I just got back to shore. I've still got to move the load before I can leave. It'll be well after dark before I get there."

"Ok" answered Black "I'll be here waiting for you. Just get the lead out and hurry up. That shipment has to go to D.C. tonight."

Ray moved the package and shrimp from the boat to the truck. He pulled the truck beside the house and went inside to wash up. There was a message on his answering machine. It was Joe telling him to bring two pair of rubber gloves, some rags, and a gallon of Clorox with him. Whatever Joe was planning sure sounded strange. He got the things and put them in the truck. Next he went into his bedroom and got his pistol and holster out of his gun cabinet. His pistol was a Colt 45 automatic; he would keep it very close for a while just in case there were any surprises. Then he entered Joe's bedroom. Joe's bow and quiver of arrows was in a corner of the room. He gathered them up and laid them on the bed. Next he got Joe's boots and a change of cloths from his closet. He carried everything out to the truck and headed for Wilmington. Both brothers were accomplished deer hunters. They both preferred the bow and arrow to the gun. It was much more challenging.

Ray knew a little about the Southside Motel. It was a place where everybody minded their own business and the cops weren't welcome. Joe's room was on the very end of the building. It was the best room in the place if you wanted some privacy. Ray parked the truck and knocked on the door. Joe opened the door and let him in.

"Did you get everything?" said Joe.

"Yeah, I got everything you told me to get," answered Ray "what the hell are we going to do?"

"I've been thinking about this the whole time I've been gone," answered Joe "we need to kill Black without anybody knowing it. We don't want the cops asking a bunch of questions. I've thought of a way to make it look like he killed himself. We'll also make sure his body is never found. Ok, here's what we're going to do; it's got to be real dark before we go to Black's place. If he's not alone we'll wait until later to get him. If he's by himself, when he goes in the truck to check the package, I'll slip in the side door and put an arrow in him. It'll be real quiet so nobody in the neighborhood will know anything's going on. Then we'll put his body in the back of your truck and clean our prints off everything. Your truck's got a camper shell on it, so we can hide his body. We'll throw the dope in with his body. On the way out of town we'll stop and call the D.C. cops. We'll tell them that W & W seafood is a front for drugs. We'll tell them a man named Amos Black owns it, and Black also owns a big warehouse in Wilmington, North Carolina. He has a truck with a hidden compartment in it that he uses to move the dope from Wilmington to Washington. Washington is where all the money's at. They better raid the place right away because Black is getting scared and is ready to leave the country. Hopefully they'll find some dope in the D.C. store and arrest Pete. I'm sure the D.C. cops will call the Wilmington cops and tell them about Black. Then the Wilmington cops will raid the warehouse down here. On the way to Black's place we'll stop and buy two shovels, two flashlights, and a tarp. We'll hide Black's body in the tarp and take it out to Green Swamp and bury it. We'll throw the package in the hole with him. I don't want anything to do with dope after tonight. I'll follow you in Black's car. After we bury him, we'll take his car and leave it parked on the high-rise bridge. We'll clean it up first; even take the license plate and vehicle identification number off. That will keep everybody concentrating on the car. Meanwhile everyone will think the driver has jumped off the bridge and committed suicide. It'll take the cops a while to find out who owns the car. They'll eventually trace it to Black. When it turns out he's missing, everyone will think he's the one who committed suicide. By then everybody will know about Black being a dope dealer. They'll also know that the cops raided both his warehouses. Everyone will think Black knew the cops were closing in on him and he started to run. They'll think he got as far as Oak Island and just decided to end it all. He's not the kind of guy that would last long in prison. People will think he cleaned the car up so the cops wouldn't know he was the one they were searching for."

"Why don't we just throw his body off of the bridge?"

"If someone finds him they'll see he was shot with an arrow and the cops will start a murder investigation. If they just find his car, Holder and his deputies might do a short investigation, but it won't be much to it. Besides we can't just throw the dope in the water, it's in a waterproof package."

"We could punch holes in the package and throw the dope off of the bridge."

"We could, but if we throw the package in the waterway, it'd be our luck some fisherman would reel it in and give it to the cops. The last thing we want is the cops asking a lot of questions. The best thing we can do is leave it in the swamp with Black's body. Everyone has to think Black committed suicide by jumping off the bridge. If his body's never found in the ocean it won't be that unusual. If the cops believe he jumped off that bridge they won't spend much time looking for his body. I want to make sure the son of a bitch is never found. I want his body to rot in the swamp. After everything's over we'll come back to my motel room. We sure don't want to be seen driving on the island at that time of the morning. We'll wait until well after noon before we go home. Remember we're celebrating my last trip. If anybody asks, we'll say we went to a couple of bars then we stayed in the motel bar until we were both drunk. That way we wouldn't have to drive. We sure don't have to worry about anyone at this motel telling the cops anything."

"It's not going to be any fun walking around in that swamp at night," remarked Ray "with all the snakes and gators in there it'll even be dangerous."

"Hell Ray, we've been in the swamp at night before. We used to poach deer in there at night. I know that was a long time ago, but there's nothing in there now that wasn't in there then. That's why I had you bring my boots. I see you're already wearing yours."

"What about the truck? People on the island know I use one of Black's trucks every now and then. If the cops find the one with the hidden compartment you think they'll ask me any questions?

"All Black's trucks look the same. None of them have any markings on them. If anybody asks you about the truck just say you don't know anything about a hidden compartment. Say that Black let you use one of his trucks so you could take your shrimp straight to him when you get in. Say it was a good deal for both of you. Besides you're not the only fisherman that uses one of his trucks."

That was true. After all Black was in the seafood business. He would often let fishermen use one of his trucks so they could bring their catch straight to him and it would be as fresh as possible. Black would go to any length to beat out the other dealers.

"You don't think you'll have a problem shooting Black with an arrow?"

"I've been building up hate for that bastard for the past two months. Just thinking about him putting his filthy hands on the girls makes my blood boil. It'll be a joy to put an arrow in him. Like I said it'd be just like killing a great big pig. I won't have a bit of trouble killing him. If we bury him deep in Green Swamp we sure won't have to worry about anybody finding him. The main thing is we'll have to do all this without anybody seeing us. I'm sure nobody's going to be in the swamp tonight. It'll be close to daylight before we get to the bridge, at this time of the year, there shouldn't be any traffic. If we do meet a car on the bridge we'll just keep driving into town and turn around. You follow far enough behind so nobody would think we're together."

Ray was convinced, "Ok let's do it, it's pitch dark outside now, so we better get started, but remember we'll only act if Black is alone in the warehouse."

"That's right, if we don't get him tonight we'll get him later."

Joe sat on the bed and put his boots on. Then they drove to a nearby hardware store and bought the shovels, flashlights and tarp. Next they drove to W & W Seafood. They stopped by Ray's truck and put the shovels, lights and tarp in the back. Then Ray drove around back to the roll up door. He went in the side door to open the roll up door. Joe slid out of the truck with his bow and quiver of arrows and stood beside the building. When Ray got the door open he pulled the truck inside and closed the door behind him. Next he backed the truck up but stopped well short of the bin. Amos Black came walking toward him.

"It's about damn time," growled Black "I was about ready to come looking for you. You've shot my schedule all to hell."

"I know," answered Ray "but I couldn't help it. You here all by yourself?"

"You don't think I would pay anybody else to wait on your sorry ass do you," growled Black again.

"I got here as fast as I could. My boats getting old: things are starting to break on her. That damn fuel pumps going to cost me a fortune. It sure wasn't any fun sitting out there waiting for a boat to tow me in."

“My heart just bleeds for you,” replied Black “with all the money you make from me you’ll soon be able to buy a new boat. You go up front while I unload the truck and check the package then I’ll come up and pay you.”

“There’s not enough shrimp to fool with. That’s why I didn’t back all the way up to the bin. Just check your package and I’ll be on my way. You can have the shrimp.” Ray walked toward the front of the building; he looked back and saw Black climb in the back of the truck with a shovel. There was no way Black could see Joe slip in the side door and creep up to the truck. Joe walked silently beside the truck and peeked in the back. Black was bent over taking a screw out of the floor. He was facing toward the front of the truck. Joe notched an arrow and moved to the center of the doorway directly behind Black. He pulled the bowstring back and waited a second. Black raised his head a little and Joe let the arrow fly. The arrow hit Black in the center of his neck and went all the way through him. His body fell forward, jerked a few times, and then lay still. Joe waited a second then climbed in the truck and kicked Black’s body. Amos Black was dead. Ray appeared at the back of the truck.

“Look at that shot,” bragged Joe “I got him right in the middle of the neck. He didn’t even bleed much. I told you it’d be just like shooting a great big pig.”

“That was a hell of a good shot,” replied Ray “I can’t believe you could hold the bow steady enough to shoot like that. I’m so nervous I’d probably have shot myself.”

“It’s all in the mind. You know how determined I am when I decide to do something.”

“Now it’s time for us to get busy. We’ve got to get rid of anything that’ll show we’ve been here tonight.”

Ray opened the roll up door and brought his truck inside, then he closed the door behind him. He backed his truck beside the seafood truck. They spread the tarp on the truck's bed and went in the refrigerated truck to get Black's body. Ray picked him up by the shoulders and Joe got his feet.

"This ain't going to be easy," said Joe

"Yeah" replied Ray "he's got to weight over three hundred pounds. Be careful you don't pull a muscle or strain your back. We've still got to take him out in the swamp."

"I know," answered Joe "I'm not looking forward to dragging his fat ass around in that swamp."

They finally got Black's body carried out and laid it on the tarp in Ray's truck. They took his keys out of his pocket; they also took all the money out of his billfold. They figured if they were going to murder him they might as well rob him to. Ray got the package out and covered the hidden compartment up with ice and shrimp. He threw the package beside Black's body. Then they put on the rubber gloves, took some rags, and Clorox, and started cleaning. They cleaned up Black's blood, they cleaned everything in the truck, and they cleaned everything in the building that they had touched. When they finished they threw the dirty rags on Black's body. They covered him with the tarp and locked the camper door. Ray opened the roll up door, and drove his truck out, then closed the door back. He made sure both doors were locked. Joe got in Black's car and followed Ray onto the street. They went a few blocks then pulled into a shopping center. Ray used a pay phone and called the D.C. cops. He placed his handkerchief over the mouthpiece and told the officer that answered to put him through to someone in narcotics. Captain James Moorefield answered the call.

"Listen up," said Ray "I'm not going to tell you my name or where I'm calling from. There's a seafood store in D.C. called W & W Seafood. A man named Amos Black owns it. Black uses this store as a front for drugs. He also owns a big warehouse in Wilmington, North Carolina. He has a truck with a hidden compartment in the bed that is used to haul the drugs from Wilmington to D.C. He gets a hell of a lot more money selling the stuff in D.C. then he would get in Wilmington. Black is starting to worry about getting caught. He's made a ton of money, and he's planning to take it, and leave town tonight. He might even leave the country. If you want to catch him you better act right away."

Then he hung up the phone. He got back in his truck and continued driving out of the city. Joe was right behind him in Black's car.

CHAPTER 7

Captain James Moorefield was used to getting anonymous phone calls about dope dealers. He decided a long time ago to just let the caller talk as long as they were willing to. The more they talked the more apt they would be to let valuable information slip out. His phone also printed out the number of the person calling. That information was usually useless; nobody uses their own phone to make an anonymous phone call. He took a lot of notes during the phone calls. He also had a tape recorder on his phone that he switched on as soon as he knew what the call was about. He seldom played the tape, his notes were usually all the information he needed. As soon as Ray hung up the phone Captain Moorefield went into action. He called his second in command, Lieutenant Jim Hartford, into his office.

"Jim" he said "I just got a tip about a possible drug dealer in our city. What do you know about a place called W & W Seafood and the owner Amos Black?"

"W & W Seafood's over on Meade Avenue," replied Hartford "we don't get many complaints about drugs from that part of town. As far as I know the store's a legitimate business. I don't know anything about Amos Black. The names not familiar, I'm sure we've never arrested him."

"Ok, have our nearest squad car check out the place, and see if anybody's over there. If anybody's there detain them until we get there. Have a search warrant drew up for the place, and make sure you double-check the address. I don't want any screw-ups. The caller said Black also owns a warehouse in Wilmington, North Carolina, so he might live down there. See if we've got an address for him if not find out who manages the place and get an address. While you're doing that I'll get a squad ready to raid the place. The caller said Black was ready to run so we better act fast. I want everything ready to move in twenty minutes."

Twenty minutes later Moorefield had a squad of eight men and a search warrant. Hartford told him that Amos Black had no address in Washington. The store was managed by a man named Dewey Caldwell who lived at 1032 East Baker Street, just six blocks from the store. Moorefield took two officers and headed for Caldwell's house. He told Hartford to take the rest of the men and waited for him at W & W Seafood.

It was eleven o'clock at night, and Dewey Caldwell had just climbed into bed. He had put in a long day at work and he was bone tired. Suddenly someone was ringing his doorbell. Who the hell could that be at this time of night he thought. The last thing in the world he wanted was company. He crawled out of bed and put his pants back on. Then he went to his front door and looked through the peephole. He was surprised to see a man and two police officers standing there. The only thing he could think of was that somebody must have broken into the store. He opened the door and said, "is there a problem officers?"

"Yeah" answered Moorefield "we need you to come with us to the seafood store. We've got a warrant to search the place."

"Search for what?"

"Search for drugs, now come on and let's go."

"Drugs, at W & W Seafood that's ridiculous. There are no drugs at that store. The only things in there are fish and shrimp. You guys must have the wrong place."

"We don't have time to fool around, bring the key, and get out here before we come in and get you."

Moorefield was beginning to get agitated. He hated to waste time.

"Ok, I'll come and unlock the place for you, search all you want, but you won't find any drugs there. I've worked there ever since the place opened. I guarantee you guys you're wasting your time. Give me a few minute's to put on a shirt and some shoes. "

Caldwell came out and got in the car with Moorefield. They arrived at the seafood store a short time later. Hartford and the rest of the men were waiting for them. They showed Caldwell the search warrant before he opened the front door.

"Ok guys," said Moorefield "I want everything in here searched from top to bottom. Look in the fish, under the fish, and under the ice. Look for any hidden places, anywhere they might hide dope. We're not leaving until every square inch of this place has been searched."

He turned to Caldwell and asked, "how many trucks you got here?"

"Just two, parked in the back," answered Caldwell.

"The caller said one of the trucks had a hidden compartment in it"

"I don't have the slightest idea what you're talking about. Why would one of our trucks have a hidden compartment in it?"

“To move the dope from Wilmington to Washington. You know Black’s got a big seafood warehouse down there don’t you?”

“Sure I do,” answered Caldwell “we get trucks from that warehouse all the time.”

“Apparently he brings the dope in down there, then sends it up here hidden in a truck. We‘ve got more addicts in Washington than they have down there. If he gets drugs into the city he‘ll have plenty of customers.”

“This is all screwed up. I’m telling you there have never been any drugs at this store.”

“We’ll see about that,” replied Moorefield "you just stay out of our way and let us search."

Then he shouted to Hartford, “Jim take a couple of guys and check every square inch of those trucks. The hidden compartments suppose to be in the bed somewhere.”

Caldwell watched in bewilderment as the cops tore the store apart. They checked in, over, and under everything in the place. It soon looked like a tornado had gone through the place. Fish, shrimp, and ice were thrown all over the floor. Paper was spread out all over the office. Every drawer in Caldwell’s desk had been emptied. Caldwell was something of a neat freak, before he went home each day he made sure the place was neat and tidy. Seeing the store in such a mess nearly brought tears to his eyes. Two hours later not a single ounce of dope had been found. Neither of the trucks had a hidden compartment in it. Moorefield called Hartford to the front of the store.

“If this guy Blacks got any dope it must be in Wilmington” he said “either that or somebody’s jerking us around. Call off the search, and send the guy’s back to their regular duties.”

He turned to Caldwell and said, “Mr. Caldwell we’re sorry to have bothered you. We didn’t find any dope here, but the owners still not off the hook. I understand Amos Black lives in Wilmington, North Carolina. We’ll have the cops down there check his place out. I’ll have Jim take you back home.”

Caldwell replied, “you guys just going to leave the store in this mess? It looks like a bomb went off in here.”

“Sorry” replied Moorefield “we don’t have the time to put everything in its proper place. I’ve got to get these men back on patrol. We’ve still got a city to protect.”

Caldwell turned to Hartford and said, “don’t worry about taking me home. I’ll be here the rest of the night cleaning up the mess you guys made. Just take your search warrant and go.”

When Moorefield got back to his office he called the Wilmington police department. He talked to Captain Jason Knight.

“There’s a seafood store in your city named W & W Seafood,” said Moorefield “it’s run by a man named Amos Black.”

“That’s right,” replied Knight “I know Mr. Black very well. He's one of Wilmington's most respected business men.”

“Black also owns a store up here,” said Moorefield “I got an anonymous phone call telling me that he uses these stores as a front for drugs. Apparently he brings the drugs into the port down there, and then trucks them up here to sell. One of his trucks is suppose to have a compartment hidden in the bed. We just raided his store up here. There were no drugs found in it and no truck with a compartment in it. Maybe somebody’s just pissed off at Black and jerking us around. It wouldn't be the first time somebody gave us a phony tip. You guys might want to check out the store down there."

"I don't see how anybody could get drugs into the State Port down here. The Coast Guard and DEA are always checking the ships when they come in. I appreciate you calling though, we'll sure look into it."

When Captain Knight hung up the phone he called his night sergeant into his office and told him about the call.

"I've known Amos Black a long time," he said "I can't believe he would be dealing drugs. He's one of the city's most prosperous businessmen. I think somebody's just screwing with us. We don't have enough people to raid the warehouse now anyway. Have a car go over to W & W Seafood and stake the place out until morning. If anybody tries to come in or leave the place have him or her detained and call me. When the day shift comes in we'll raid the place. I'll have a warrant ready by then. I'll be very surprised if we find any dope though."

Wilmington Chief of Police William W. Calhoun came to work at seven that morning. Captain Knight met him at his office door. He told him about the call from the Washington Police. He also handed him a search warrant for W & W Seafood.

"Good work," said Calhoun "I'll get ten deputies before they go on patrol, and we'll raid the place. We're lucky enough to have one of the best drug-sniffing dogs in the state. If there's any drugs out there old Blue will find them. You care to hang around, and go with me to Black's house?"

“I sure do,” replied Knight “Amos Black is a friend of mine. I think somebody's trying to set him up. I‘ve had the warehouse staked out ever since the call came in. Nobody has tried to enter or leave the place.”

The chief sent the officers to the warehouse while he and Knight went to Black’s house. When they got there, they noticed there were no vehicles parked in the driveway. They rang the doorbell for ten minutes but nobody answered it.

“That’s strange,” remarked Knight as they were leaving “Blacks not at home or at the warehouse. The Washington Police didn’t say anything about him being up there. I wonder where he’s at?”

“I don’t know,” replied Calhoun “but we’ve got a search warrant, that’s all we need to legally get in the warehouse.”

The raiding party was waiting for them at W & W Seafood. They informed the chief that the building was locked tight. The chief ordered the small door beside the roll up door to be knocked open. Sledgehammers made quick work of the door. Once inside, the chief pretty much gave the same commands the Washington police had gave for the store up there.

“Search in the fish, under the fish, under the ice, in the office, and any place that dope could be hidden” he ordered "make sure old Blue runs his nose over every inch of the place."

There were eight trucks parked in the building.

“Captain Knight take four men, and start going through those trucks,” ordered the chief.

Knight grabbed the four officers that were closest to him and headed for the trucks.

"There's suppose to be a compartment hidden in the bed of a truck," he said, "the bad news is all of them have probably got fish, or shrimp, and ice in them. You'll have to get some shovels and throw the contents in the bins. We've got to check the floor of each truck. You officers split up into two groups and check the back while I check in the front."

The police were just getting started good when a car pulled into the parking lot. A short white haired lady got out and walked over to the broken down door.

"What in the world are you guys doing in there?" she asked

The chief walked over to her and asked, "who are you lady?"

"My name is Shirley Clayton," she replied "I'm Mr. Black's secretary."
The chief responded, "do you know where Mr. Black is?"

"He's always here by this time of the morning. What's going on here?"

"We got a call saying Black uses this place and the store in Washington to deal drugs. We've got a warrant to search the warehouse."

"Oh good gracious," replied Clayton "I've worked for Mr. Black for nine years. I know he's not mixed up in any drug business."

"So you've never saw any drugs here."

"Of course not," she answered "Mr. Black wouldn't do anything like that."

"Would you know cocaine if you saw it?"

"It's some kind of white powder. I guess it looks like flour."

"Have you ever seen anything that looks like flour here?"

"The only thing I've ever seen here is seafood."

"How many people work here?"

“Three men work in the warehouse, and we have six drivers. They’ll all come to work in another hour.”

“Are all your trucks here?”

“Yes, we have eight trucks here and two in Washington. The drivers rotate the trucks. The full ones will go to different stores throughout the city. The empty ones will go to the docks to load up fresh seafood.”

“That’s good, I wanted to make sure we didn’t miss searching any.”

“You think one of the trucks has dope in it?” asked Clayton.

“Have you ever seen inside the back of the trucks?”

“I’m a secretary. I work in the office. I don’t have any reason to look in the trucks.”

“You have no idea where Mr. Black is?”

“No, I’ve never known him to be late before. You think something has happened to him?”

“All I can say is we’ve got a warrant, and I intend to search this entire store and everything in it” replied the chief “we went by Black’s house this morning. His car was gone, and nobody would answer the door. Now you don’t know where he’s at. I have to think that somebody from Washington tipped him off about our raid, and he took off running. You go up to the office with one of our officers, and open anything that’s locked up. I’ll let you know when we’re finished back here. I‘ll leave a couple officers at the gate to question the other employees when they come in.”

An hour later the cops had pretty much searched the entire warehouse. Captain Knight and his men were searching the last truck. Knight was going through the glove compartment when one of the officers in the back shouted for him. Knight went around the truck and climbed into the back.

"We found something," said one of the officers "there's a steel plate here held in place by four screws."

Knight remembered seeing a screwdriver in the glove compartment. He got it and began taking the screws out. When he finished with the screws he stuck the screwdriver under the plate and lifted it up. Under the plate was an empty compartment.

"This is definitely the compartment we've been looking for," said Knight "one of you go get the chief."

One of the officers left the truck and walked over to the chief. He told the chief what they had found in the back of the truck. The chief immediately went over to the truck and climbed into the back.

"That looks like an ideal place to hide drugs," said the chief. "The caller was right about the compartment being in a truck. If he was telling the truth about that, then everything he said was probably true."

"Have you found any drugs in the warehouse?" asked Knight.

"No" answered the chief "not even anything that looks like a drug. Old Blue didn't even pick up a scent. The guys are finishing up now. We've still got to question the other employees when they come in. Of course, I don't expect any of them to admit they helped deal drugs. When we get back to the station, I'm going to put out an all points bulletin on Amos Black. He's got a lot of questions to answer. Even though we didn't find any drugs, I want him to explain the compartment in the truck and everything else the caller told us. I've got a feeling the son of a bitch has already run off."

CHAPTER 8

While the cops were responding to Ray's phone call the brothers had been busy themselves. They drove out of the city and headed for Green Swamp. They drove very carefully; making sure the cops had no reason to stop them. If anybody saw what was in the back of Ray's truck everything was blew to hell. The swamp is located ten miles inland from Oak Island. Walk a hundred feet out in Green Swamp, and you'll feel like you've gone back in time a thousand years. It's hard to imagine that most of the East Coast once looked like this. There are thousands of acres containing nothing but wetlands, pine trees, scrub brush and just plain mud, and muck. It's not like the swamps you see on TV, full of slimly water and cypress trees. It's more like a giant mud puddle full of scrub brush, and thickets, with a pine tree ever now and then. There are spots of dry land and spots where the water is over four feet deep. There are also sinkholes full of quicksand. If a man steps in one of them he'll soon vanish from the face of the earth. Small animals, deer, turkey and black bears are common sights in the swamp. You won't see many bobcats, alligators, rattlesnakes, or cottonmouth water moccasins, but they're in there. They're usually deep in the swamp and not very active in the daytime. Green Swamp is not a place to be wandering around in, especially at night.

Not only is the swamp dangerous it also stinks like hell. It's full of stagnant water, rotting trees, rotting leaves and pine needles, and dead animals. Anyone who has smelled rotten eggs has a good idea of the way the swamp stinks.

One paved road cuts right through the middle of the swamp. Coming off the paved road every couple of miles are dirt roads leading deep into the swamp. Years ago the timber company used these dirt roads to harvest the pine trees. Today most of the swamp is held in a preserve. Thanks to some environmental action, the swamp will always stay the way it is now. Ray and Joe have been deer hunting in the swamp every since they were young boys. Most of the land is posted 'No Hunting' but that never stopped them. They know their way around the swamp well enough to even poach deer there at night, although they hadn't done it in a long time. Ray drove his truck up the paved road until he was in the middle of the swamp then he turned onto one of the dirt roads. Joe, driving Black's BMW, was right behind him. They drove about a mile down the dirt road and stopped. Joe left the BMW and got in Ray's truck. They drove deeper and deeper into the swamp. The road got so bad that only a four-wheel drive could go on it. The mud puddles seemed big enough to swallow the truck whole. They just kept going until the truck wouldn't go any farther. They stopped in what seemed like the middle of a jungle. They weren't lost though; both of them had hunted in this area before. They each got a flashlight and got out of the truck. Then they opened the camper door and pulled down the tailgate. Each of them grabbed a side of the tarp and pulled. After much effort the tarp, and its contents, slid off the truck onto the ground. Holding a light and a shovel in one hand and the tarp in the other they started dragging the tarp through the swamp. It was tough going, the ground was muddy, and Black's body was very heavy. The mud and muck came over their boots making them fall down often. In the darkness they couldn't see all the tree limbs and they kept slapping them in the face and eyes. Thorns kept scratching any part of their body that wasn't covered up. Plus they had to check in front before they took each step. They knew how dangerous the swamp could be at night. One wrong step and a sinkhole could swallow you up. There was also the danger of stepping right on top of an alligator or water moccasin.

"After this I'm going to look like I've been picking blackberries in a thorn patch," said Joe

"I know," replied Ray "we should have had enough sense to have brought some coveralls. Thank God we've got on boots. Could you imagine going through this mess with shoes on?"

"Not while dragging this heavy son of a bitch. "

"I'm sure we'll never have to bring another body out here."

"It's tempting to just leave him right here and let the gators eat him. I guess we'd better bury him though. We can't afford to take any chances."

After slipping and sliding about a hundred feet Joe said, "let's take a break."

"OK" replied Ray "I need to stop. I've got so much sweat dropping in my eyes I can hardly see. We'll look around the swamp while we catch our breath."

They spent several minutes, shinning their lights forward, looking for a spot clear enough to bury Black.

"I don't see a place clear enough to dig in," said Joe "we'll have to keep going."

"Let's take the fat bastard on out in the swamp," answered Ray.

After tugging forward for another hundred feet they reached a small clearing.

“This looks good,” said Ray.

“I’ve gone about as far as I can,” answered Joe “this will have to be the place.” They took the shovels, and moved the leaves and pine needles back, then started digging. They dug at a furious pace. They were in a hurry to get Black's body in the ground and put the dope business behind them forever. The ground was wet and loose, except for all the roots, digging was easy.

“This sure gives me an eerie feeling,” said Ray “with the only light coming from our flashlights lying on the ground. I can see fog rising up from around Black’s body.”

“What's the matter,” replied Joe “you afraid the swamp thing is hiding out here somewhere?”

“It’s not that, it’s just that I’ve never buried a body before. In my wildest dreams I never thought I’d be burying one in the middle of a swamp, in the middle of the night. Especially one that I helped kill.”

“I’m the one that killed him, and I don’t regret it one bit,” replied Joe “I will be glad to get the fat bastard in the ground though. Let‘s just hope all this work is worth it. If we get caught after all this trouble they can throw me under the jailhouse.”

They dug and dug until the hole was nearly over their heads. Finally when the hole was about six feet deep they climbed out. They pulled the tarp over the hole and let it slid in. Black’s body, the package and the dirty rags all went in the hole with the tarp. Working at the same furious pace they had when digging it, they filled the hole with dirt. The brothers were eager to get everything over with and get out of the swamp. After they had all the dirt in it they spread the leaves and pine needles over it. When they finished, it looked like just a mound of dirt.

“You reckon we should say a few words over him” said Ray

“What the hell could we say,” replied Joe “well Lord, here’s one fat pig that got exactly what he deserved: amen.”

“Come on Joe, we just killed a man and buried his body. Show some respect for the dead.”

“Ok, how about this: Lord I’m sure you’ve done judged Black and the pigs roasting in hell now.“

“Very funny,” said Ray “if you can’t be serious lets get the hell out of here.“ They both knew the package was worth a lot of money but they didn’t know where to sell it. Besides after tonight they were through with the dope business. They returned to the truck and drove back to Black’s car. With the rubber gloves on they took some rags, and Clorox, and wiped the car clean. Then they cleaned out the glove compartment, and trunk, and put the contents in Ray’s truck. Ray took his knifepoint and scratched the vehicle identification number off. Next they took all the screws out of the license plate but one, which they left just tight enough to hold the plate on.

“With no prints or license plate, it’ll take the cops a while to find out whose car this is,” said Joe “that’s just what we want. Everybody will be thinking about the car and the ocean. Nobody will think about Green Swamp.”

“This better work,” replied Ray “we sure can’t bring ol Black back from the dead.”

"I wouldn't bring him back even if I could. He's right where he ought to be: burning in hell."

When they finished with the car, Ray followed Joe as they drove to Oak Island. It was near four in the morning when they reached the high-rise bridge. They hadn't seen a single car the whole trip. Joe parked the car at the top of the bridge and removed the license plate, while Ray turned his truck around.

"Let's get the hell out of here," shouted Joe as he jumped in the passenger side of Ray's truck. They headed back to Joe's motel room.

"Well" said Ray "you think we pulled it off ok?"

"Yeah" answered Joe "at this time of the morning nobody's driving around here. If we can just get back to the motel without anybody noticing us we should be ok. I just hope the cops find the car before somebody runs into it."

"If anybody drives up on the bridge, they'll see the car in plenty of time to stop before they reach it."

"They should, of course anyone driving at this time of the morning might be half asleep."

"If I ever do anything like this again I'm sure I'll have a nervous breakdown" replied Ray.

Half an hour later they pulled into the motel parking lot. They hadn't passed any cars until they were just outside of the city limits. There was just enough traffic in the city to keep them from standing out. They went in the room, took a shower, and went to bed. The next trip out to sea they would get rid of the license plate and contents of Black's car.

They woke around noon, put on clean cloths, and went to a local restaurant for lunch. Then they headed for Oak Island. As they approached the high-rise bridge, they noticed quite a few people standing on it. People were looking down at the water and pointing in all different directions.

"You can sure tell something's going on," said Ray "all these people must be looking for Black's body. His cars been moved."

"Let's just hope the cops have it at the impound lot," said Joe.

"I don't know where else it could be. The lots behind the police station, so we won't be able to see the car. We'll go by there and see if anything exciting going on." Before they got to the police station they could tell something big was happening. There were cars parked everywhere and lots of people standing around talking.

"That's got to be it," said Joe "don't stop. Let's just go home and get some sleep. We don't want anybody to see us here."

The brothers went home and got some more sleep. That evening they were eager for the news to come on TV. The lead story was about a car found abandoned on the Oak Island Bridge. At the time police didn't know who owned the car or where the driver was. The car had no license plate and no fingerprints were found on it. The police could only assume the driver jumped off of the bridge. The local rescue squad has been patrolling the waterway and for a few miles out in the ocean, looking for a body. So far the search has turned up nothing. This story was followed be a report on a drug raid at a local seafood warehouse. The report said the Wilmington police raided W & W Seafood early that morning. They had found no drugs. That was all the report said.

"Either they didn't find the compartment in the truck, or they're not telling everything," said Ray

"I know," answered Joe "we should hear more about it tomorrow. Sometimes the cops don't tell the press everything they know for awhile. "

It was about time for the girls to get home from work. The brothers took a shower, put on nice cloths, and went to the girl's apartment. Mona opened the door for them. She threw her arms around Joe and gave him a big kiss.

"Are you home for good now?" She asked

"That's right babe," he answered "I'm all through with the ship. From now on I'll stay close to land and close to you. I'll be a land lover for the rest of my life."

"I like that idea a lot," she said "I just can't believe you gave up your job so we could be together. I've never loved you more than I do right now. In fact, I may never let go of you."

Joe didn't give her a chance to say anything else. He gave her one long kiss after another. Ray walked in and gave Carol a big kiss also.

"It's time to celebrate," he said "we said goodbye to the guys last night now we're all yours."

"That's fine with me," answered Carol "we've been waiting for you."

Since the girls had to work the next day they decided to just stay at the apartment, cook some burgers, and have a few beers. They watched some TV and sat around and talked. Carol asked Ray, "did you guys hear about all the excitement on the island this morning?"

"Yeah" he replied "we saw it on the news before we came over here. It looks like some idiot jumped off the bridge and committed suicide. Whoever it was left their car parked on top of the bridge. Can you imagine someone leaving a new BMW parked on top of that bridge? I bet Chief Holder and his boys are walking on air, to have something exciting happen at this time of the year."

"Who in the world could it have been?" Asked Carol

"I don't know," answered Ray "some fool looking for a quick way to end it all I suppose. Whoever it was must have had some money to afford a car like that."

Ray was surprised at how calm he was. Of course his mind had rehearsed everything he would say many times.

"This is the biggest thing to happen on Oak Island since the last hurricane," said Joe "they'll probably never find the driver's body. Not as strong as that current is. He might be two miles out in the ocean or been ate by fish. I hate to change the subject, but I don't want to think about the ocean tonight. I just want to enjoy being home."

Mona went over and sat on Joe's lap and said, "it's good to have you home. I'll make sure you forget about everything but me tonight."

She grabbed his hand and they went into her bedroom. Carol took Ray's hand and the two of them went into her bedroom also.

Since the girls had to get up early the next day, the brothers left at eleven o'clock. They all agreed to meet at the Sea Hut at seven the next night. It would be Friday, so they could spend the whole weekend together.

The next morning the brothers took the Carolina out and trawled for shrimp. They acted like it was a perfectly normal day. The only thing unusual was Ray taking his pistol on the boat with them. They caught a nice load of shrimp and sold them at the local wholesale warehouse. The owner asked Ray if he had heard about the car found on the bridge the day before.

“Yeah” answered Ray “I saw it on the news last night.”

The owner said, “I just heard on the radio that they traced the car to an Amos Black from Wilmington. He owns a big seafood warehouse up there and another one in Washington D.C. I've heard of Amos Black. I know some fishermen around here will sometimes sell their fish and shrimp to him. Have you ever met Black?"

"Yeah, I've met Black. I've never had any dealings with him through."

"Somebody called the Washington police and told them Black was dealing dope out of his stores. The cops raided both places yesterday looking for dope. They didn’t find any dope at the Wilmington store, but they did find a truck with a hidden compartment in it. The police didn’t tell the press about the truck until they found out it was Black’s car on the bridge. They didn’t say if the D.C. cops found any dope or not. I guess Black knew the cops were about to catch him so he ran. The cops have an all points bulletin out on him. They’re never going to find him though, because his bodies in the ocean, if there’s anything left of it. I don’t know why he’d come all the way down here to commit suicide through?”

“Maybe there was too much traffic in Wilmington,” answered Ray “maybe he just headed south, got this far, and decided not to run anymore. I’m surprised somebody hasn’t jumped off that bridge before now. It’s the perfect place to commit suicide. Especially if you don’t care if your body’s never found.”

“I guess you’re right,” replied the owner “I‘ve never really thought about it, but if you wanted to vanish that‘d be a good place to do it.”

While heading back home Ray said, “I guess the cats out of the bag now. Everybody knows the car belonged to Amos Black. It took them a while to tie the car and Black‘s disappearance together just like you thought it would.”

“That’s ok,” replied Joe “people think he jumped off the bridge just like we hoped they would. Everybody thinks his body‘s lost out in the ocean somewhere or been eaten by the sharks. I would like to know what the Washington cops found though.”

“Me to,” replied Ray “I guess if they find some dope up there it’s no big deal. Pete’s got to know they raided the store down here and found the truck with the hidden compartment in it. If the cops didn’t get him, I don’t think he’ll come near this place. He's probably out of the country by now.”

All over the island people were speculating about the car and Amos Black. Like the brothers had planned most people thought Black knew the cops were about to catch him for dealing dope, and he decided to run. He got as far as Oak Island and just decided to end it all. He didn’t want the cops to know who he was so he cleaned up his car to delay them. Maybe he had a partner he wanted to buy some time for. People came up with all kinds of scenarios that would support their point of view.

The brothers were right proud of themselves. They had fooled everybody. Everybody thought Black had jumped off the bridge, and been eaten by fish, or just washed out to sea. All their hard work had paid off. Nobody even thought about looking for Black anywhere but in the ocean. People disappear in the ocean all the time. When Black’s body hadn’t been found after about a week, they figured the whole mess would die down. Oak Island would return to the same calm and peaceful place it had always been.

CHAPTER 9

The guys were at the Sea Hut promptly at seven that night. The girls hadn't got there yet so they got a table and ordered two beers. The girls arrived a few minutes later. The two couples had a good time at the bar. As they usually did they drank beer, shot pool, and danced to the music on the jukebox. They would all be able to sleep late the next day, so they stayed at the bar until after midnight. When they were ready to leave the guys said they had to run by the store and pick up some beer. They told the girls to wait ten minutes then meet them at their house. They wanted to make sure the house was safe before the girls got there. They approached the house with caution, they drove by the driveway, then Joe walked back and checked everything out before he motioned Ray to come on in. They still didn't know if anyone would come looking for them. If Black's friends in D.C. knew who they were, they could be on the island by now. When the girls arrived each couple went straight to bed. They woke late in the morning. It was Saturday, and the girls wanted to do something different that night. They wanted to go to Myrtle Beach and go to a nightclub. They could each get motel rooms, so they could stay out late and not have to worry about driving back to the island. They could go down there early and use the motel pool until night. The guys thought it was a great idea. The girls went back to their apartment and packed a few things. The guys each packed a small bag and met the girls at their apartment at noon. Since Carol had the biggest car she got the privilege of driving everybody around. That was all right with her, she wouldn't drink much anyway. She knew Joe and Mona wanted to make up for lost time, and Ray just wanted to relax. They were all in a great mood during the drive down to the beach. It had been a long time since the four of them had a weekend away from Oak Island. They got to the beach and got connecting ocean front rooms. As soon as they settled in they changed into their swimsuits and went to the pool. There were still several hours of daylight left, and the sun was warm enough to set outside. After a dip in the pool it felt great letting the suns rays warm their bodies.

"I wish this would never end," said Carol

"It's just going to get better and better," replied Ray "now that Joe's home for good we'll get to see each other a lot more often."

"Thank God," answered Carol "you know I love you very much."

Ray leaned over and gave her a quick kiss.

"I know," he replied "I love you to, and I want to be with you. Everything's soon going to work out so we can always be together."

"That would be the answer to all my dreams."

As it was getting dark they went in the room, showered, dressed up, and went to a popular restaurant for supper. Then they went to the nightclub. Neither of the brothers were great dancers, but they gave it their best shot. After a couple of beers they were really moving pretty good. The fast dances were ok but they all really loved the slow ones. Holding each other close on the dance floor set a romantic mood. I wish they were all slow songs thought Ray; I could hold Carol like this forever. It was after one o'clock before they left the club. When they got back to the rooms each couple was ready to be alone and have some time for themselves.

They had to check out of the motel at eleven that morning. They got a bite to eat and went to the State Park. There is a dressing room and shower located there. They changed into their swimsuits and spread a blanket on the beach. The ocean was a little cold, but they did go out as far as their knees. Mostly the four of them lay on the blanket and soaked up the sun. After a while Joe asked Ray to walk out on the pier with him, he wanted to check out the fishing. As they walked toward the pier Joe said

"I'm going to ask Mona to marry me, right now."

Ray replied, "you mean right now, while she's lying on a blanket at the beach."

"Darn right," said Joe "what better place could there be? It'll be a great story to tell our kids someday. Just think about how romantic it'll be; proposing to her while she's lying on the beach. A beautiful day like this is perfect to ask the woman you love to marry you."

"Well, if you're going to ask Mona now, I'm going to ask Carol now. We don't have any rings, but we can stop by a jewelry store and let them look. Maybe at least one of them will find a ring they like."

Joe was grinning like a possum, "let's go back and do it," he said "I can't wait to see the look on their faces."

The brothers returned to where the girls were lying on the blanket. They both got down on one knee, picked up their girl's hand, and said together, "will you marry me?"

It took the girls a moment to realize what was happening. When it hit them they both shouted, "Yes."

It was too bad they didn't have any champagne; it was definitely a champagne moment. The brothers said they would stop by a jewelry store on the way home and let the girls check out the rings. The girls couldn't wait; they were ready to go right away. They left the beach and went to the biggest jewelry store in town. Both girls found the perfect ring for them. After buying the rings they headed for home. The brothers couldn't believe their good luck. After all their hard work, and time spent waiting, their dreams of a new life were about to come true. The next thing they wanted to do was marry the girls and move somewhere new.

It was after dark when they got back to the girl's apartment. They had a few beers and watched TV. Mostly they just wanted to be together. The next day was Monday, and the girls had to work, so at eleven o'clock Ray said, "We better go and let you girls get some sleep. I promise we'll be here right after you get home from work tomorrow."

They kissed goodnight and the brothers headed for Oak Island. They were feeling on top of the world. They still approached the house with caution, driving by first then Joe walking back and motioning Ray to drive on in.

The next morning the guys took the Carolina out and spent the day trawling for shrimp. It had been four days since they had left Black's car on the bridge. Nobody had come looking for them yet. Although they were still a little nervous, their fear was beginning to leave them. It had been great to get away and spend the weekend with the girls at the beach. For a little while they had been able to put Oak Island, Green Swamp, and Amos Black out of their minds. After waiting so long, they were finally able to ask the girls to marry them. Life just doesn't get any better than this thought Ray. They would soon marry their girls and leave Oak Island for good.

They caught a nice load of shrimp and sold them at the local warehouse. Then they hurried home. They were eager to go see the girls. They were each in their rooms getting dressed when the doorbell rang. Joe went to the front door and looked through the peephole. Deputy Bobby Young was standing outside. Joe opened the door and said, "hello Bob what brings you out this way?"

Young replied, "I'm investigating that Amos Black fellow. You know, the one whose car was found on the bridge the other night. I need to come in and ask you and Ray a few questions."

"Come on in and have a seat," replied Joe

Deputy Young came in the house and sat on the couch beside Joe. Ray walked into the room and sat in a chair across from them.

Joe asked, "What do you want to know?"

Young said, "Ray I understand you sold shrimp to Mr. Black. Sometimes you even used one of his trucks."

"That's true," replied Ray "Black paid better than the local dealer did so when I had a big catch it was worth it to drive to his place in Wilmington. Sometimes when I was catching a lot of shrimp he'd let me bring one of his trucks out here. That way I could put the shrimp straight from the boat to the truck and haul them right to Wilmington. Black was guaranteed to get the freshest shrimp possible. I know he sometimes let other fishermen use one of his trucks also."

Young said, “Yes I know, I’ve talked to other fishermen who used his trucks. One of his trucks had a compartment hid in the bed. You ever notice anything like that?”

“Every time I used his truck the bed was covered with ice. I had no reason to check under the ice.”

“When did you see Black last?

“It was Wednesday afternoon; it was the day Joe came home. I went up the day before and borrowed a truck. As you know, this is a great time of the year to catch shrimp. I told Black, Joe would be coming in the next day, and I’d bring a load of shrimp by when I came to town to pick him up.”

“Did he seem all right?”

“He was the same ol Black, always eager to get a load of fresh shrimp.”

“You got any idea why Black would drive down to Oak Island?”

“I don’t have the slightest idea. I understand his car was found in the inbound lane. I would guess he never intended to come on the island. He just figured it’d be a perfect place to disappear. I heard he even took his license plate off. I guess he didn’t want anybody searching for him for a while. You guys got any reason for him doing that?"

“I suppose it had something to do with him being in the dope business. I assume you guys didn’t know anything about him selling dope?”

“You got that right,” replied Joe

"I understand the Washington police got a phone call tipping them off about Black," Ray said "Have they got any leads about who made that call?"

"The call was made from a phone booth several blocks from Black's warehouse down here," answered Young "Nobody has the slightest clue as to who made it. The Washington police sent Wilmington a copy of the taped phone call. I've listened to it, the sound is so muffled nobody will ever recognize the voice. I have my own personal opinion as to who did it. I believe whoever was bringing the dope in for Black met him at the warehouse that night. Black probably screwed him some way. He was very mad when he left Black's place. Mad enough to turn Black in to the police. I figure this person called Washington instead of the Wilmington police the give himself time to get far away from these parts. Whoever made that call is probably somewhere on the west coast by now.

"Now I know why I'm not a policeman," remarked Joe "How in the world could you figure all that out from the little information you have?

A big grin flashed across Young's face. He was obviously pleased with himself.

"The paper said there was no dope found at either of Black's warehouses," said Ray "is that correct?"

"That's right," answered Young "legally the only thing the Wilmington police want Black for is to find out about the hidden compartment in one of his trucks. Of course, if he had nothing to hide why didn't he stick around and face the music. I'm sure Black's guilty as hell. Hauling the dope up to Washington made a lot of sense. The money there would be a lot better than down here. Black probably dropped the dope off someplace before he got to his store. That's why no dope was found there. As far as the last shipment down here, I figure Black's supplier kept it. When Black pissed him off, he called the police, and took off with the dope. Some hippie in California is probably getting high on it right now."

"You sure are good at figuring crime out," remarked Ray "I hope you're right. I'd hate to think there are any crooks still around here. California can have all the crooks and dope addicts."

"There's still a few things we don't know," replied Young "We don't know how Black got the dope in the first place. The Coast Guard and DEA swear that none of the big ships that come into port here could get any dope by them."

"I agree with them" remarked Joe "right now we're checked just about every trip. They go over the whole ship with a dog. If they check all the ships like they do ours nothings going to get by them. Of course Wilmington is right on the intercoastal waterway. They can't possibly check all the boats going up and down that. There are plenty of places south of here that drugs could come in. We have a state port and a military port here, so they keep close tabs on us. Other ports aren't checked nearly as close. They wouldn't even have to come by boat. We're not far from interstate 95, there's probably dope going up that highway every day."

“That's true," answered Young "it's a battle we can't seem to win. Black's car was found at four AM on Thursday morning. You guys happen to notice anything unusual Wednesday or Thursday?”

“Are you kidding,” answered Joe “I guess you don’t know I just made my last boat trip? I’m not going back to sea anymore. I’m going to marry my girlfriend, and I’m planning to spend plenty of time with her. I gave her a ring this past weekend. When I came home I got a motel room. Then I called Ray and told him where I was. After he left Black’s he came over to the motel. We spent the night celebrating my last trip. We hit a couple of bars then spent the rest of the time at the motel bar. We wanted to do plenty of drinking and we didn't want to drive. We didn't even want our girls along. We figured that'd be the last time just the two of us got to party. We wanted one last blow out before we settled down. You know, we were trying to do the same stupid things we did when we were twenty-one. We must have drunk until at least two AM. I woke up with the damnest hangover I've ever had. I'm definitely too old for the wild life anymore. We didn't come back home until well after noon on Thursday. We knew there were a lot of people on the bridge for some reason. We didn't know what had happened until we saw it on the news."

Deputy Young replied, "I wish more people had enough sense not to drink and drive. Just about all our bang ups involve drivers who have been drinking. I'm sorry I had to bother you guys. The chief wanted us to ask all the locals if they knew anything about Black. I think we're just wasting our time anyway. I think Black jumped off that bridge and will never be found.

"I certainly agree with you," said Ray "Black's used to being the boss. I can't picture him spending the rest of his life in prison."

"You know, nobody has claimed that car yet. It's still at the impound lot. We haven't been able to find any next of kin for Black. Did he ever talk about his family to either of you?

"Not to me" answered Ray "all we ever talked about was business. Black was only interested in making money. Of course I would only be at his place long enough to unload and weight my shrimp. I don't know anything about his personal life. He sure didn't seem like the type that would have a wife and kids somewhere."

"I only met Black one time" replied Joe "all I remember about him is that he was a very big man. He had to weight over three hundred pounds. That water must have felt like concrete when he hit it. If by some miracle he survived the fall there's no way he could have swam in that current. I think you can write Mr. Black off as being lost at sea."

Deputy Young stood up and said, "Well I'll be on my way. Congratulations on your engagement Joe. You introduced me to your girl once at the Sea Hut, you two make a nice couple."

"Thanks," replied Joe, as he walked the deputy to the door "Ray got engaged too. I hope we can have a double wedding."

"I've saw you and your girl around the island a couple of times, Ray. Congratulations to both of you," said the deputy as he walked out the door.

When Young pulled out of the driveway Joe turned to Ray and said "that went well. It doesn't sound like the cops will be looking for Black much longer. They've got no reason to believe we were partners with him. I think we'll soon be home free."

"Yeah" replied Ray "good ol Black, may the son of a bitch rest in peace. Let's go see the girls."

CHAPTER 10

The brothers had kept their guard up, but things were happening they weren't aware of. The day after Black's car was found on the bridge, a white truck with two men in it drove by their house. The truck was pulling a red Cigarette boat behind it.

Across the waterway from the brother's house is a large cove that has a public boat ramp on it. If the brothers had been more alert, they would have noticed a red Cigarette boat at the coves entrance several times. They would have noticed a man in the boat watching their house with binoculars. They would have noticed that boat when they returned from the ocean on Monday. It was still there when they left for the girl's apartment. As soon as it got dark the red Cigarette pulled up behind the Carolina. Two men got out and walked up to the house. One of them took a skeleton key out of his pocket and opened the door. They went inside and locked the door behind them.

Unaware of what was happening back at their house, the brothers and their fiancés were busy making wedding plans. None of them wanted to wait very long. They decided one weekend between Thanksgiving and Christmas would be the perfect time. The girls wanted to talk to their families before they set a definite date. They put the wedding plans aside, drank a few beers, and watched some television. Since the girls had to work the next day the brothers left their place at eleven. They arrived home feeling good; they figured if anyone were looking for them, they would have showed up by now. They still approached the house with caution. Joe got the pistol out of the glove compartment as they drove down the driveway. After the truck was parked, Joe carried the pistol with him as he walked up on the front porch. He unlocked the front door and flipped the living room light on. He walked through the doorway with Ray right behind him. Ray shut the door and both of them walked toward the center of the room. Two figures walked out of the dark kitchen and a voice says, "Hello ass holes, remember me."

The brothers were so startled they couldn't talk. Standing in front of them was Pete and the black guy from Washington; each had a pistol in his hand.

Pete said, "Drop that gun, set on the couch, and put your hands out."

Joe dropped the pistol then the brothers sat on the couch and held their hands out.

"In case your memory's weak, my name's Pete, and this guy is just called Mac," said Pete "Mac put the cuffs on them, and bring that gun over here."

The black guy took two pair of handcuffs out of his pocket. He walked over and put cuffs on each of their wrist. Then he picked up the pistol and put it on the floor next to Pete.

Then Pete said, "You two are the dumbest son of a bitches I ever met in my life. What did you think you could do, kill Black, then call the cops on us and sell the dope yourselves?"

Ray replied, "I don't know what the hell you're talking about."

"Yes you do," answered Pete "now just tell me where the dopes at and we'll finish this real quick."

Again Ray said, "I don't know what the hell you're talking about."

"Yes you do, and I guarantee you you'll tell me. Before I'm done you'll tell me everything I want to know. You boys seem to think we're playing some kind of a game here. You'll find out how serious we are when the pain starts."

Pete turned to the black guy and said "Mac get us some chairs."

The black guy brought two chairs out of the kitchen and both men sat down.

Pete said, "Which one of you is Ray?"

Ray nodded his head and said, "I'm Ray."

"You dumb ass, you know your name and address are right in the phone book. We didn't have a bit of trouble finding out where you live. I told you ass holes nobody pulls anything on us. Now you're going to pay, now you're going to be fertilizer. I don't know how you two idiots managed to get ol Black but we've got more sense than he had. You might as well make it easy on yourselves. If you go ahead and tell me where the dopes at I promise I'll make it real quick. Just one shot behind the ear. Otherwise it's going to be very painful, and you'll still tell me what I want to know."

Ray's heart was beating so fast he thought it would jump out of his chest. All he could think to say was

"Why should we tell you anything, you're going to kill us no matter what we do?"

"That's true," replied Pete "I am going to kill you, but we've got plenty of time. I'm enjoying myself watching you two squirm. Before I make you ass holes talk, I'm going to tell you just how stupid you've been. I'm going to tell you all about Black and me and how I know who you two dumb asses are."

Both brothers looked straight at Pete as he began to tell his story.

"I own a seafood warehouse in Washington," said Pete "about five years ago Black opened a store up there. It was small and outside the city so it didn't bother me any. One day, right out of the blue, Black called me up. He said he wanted to meet for lunch, said he had a business deal for me. So we met for lunch, and Black said he owned a large seafood warehouse in Wilmington. He said if I bought all my seafood from him in bulk he would give me a good price. So I started buying from Black, we had a legal business deal going on. Ol Black was one hell of a businessman. I bet you guys didn't know he owned a jewelry store right in the middle of Wilmington. He imported the stuff straight from Thailand. A few years ago he was over there buying jewelry when his dealer told him he could get some pure coke for a little of nothing. If he could figure out a way to get the stuff into the states, he could make a killing. A while later Black called me up again and we meet for lunch. He said he needed a partner, someone who knows the city well. He said he had a contact in Thailand who could get some coke cheap, and he had a plan worked out to bring it into the states. He said he'd been talking to a dumb ass fisherman and his brother about getting it to Wilmington. We would haul it from Wilmington to Washington hidden in a seafood truck. It wouldn't be much coke, but it was pure stuff. If we could get it to D.C., cut it, and deal it ourselves, we could make a small fortune. I know Mac and Jake are dealers, so we got them to help us sell the stuff. So the four of us set up a business. If you punks knew what a kilo of pure coke brings on the D.C. streets you'd know why we weren't about to get out of the business. In fact, ol Black was trying to figure out a way to bring more of the stuff in. Things went well for a couple of years, you boys bring the dope to Black, Mac and Jake drive it up to Washington, and we deal it from my store. That was my place you drove the truck to in

Washington, you wasn't even close to Black's store. When you had the cop's raid Black's store they couldn't find any dope because there had never been any there. I made sure you punks got good and lost so you could never find my place again. Anyway like I was saying: things were going good. Then I found out Jake's keeping some of our money for himself. Black and me are both businessmen, we know exactly how much money our dealers get each month. That was about the same time you punks were whining about getting out. I called up Black and told him about Jake. We came up with a plan to handle Jake and teach you ass holes a lesson at the same time. The next time Jake came down for a load, Black put a bullet in his head, and hid his body in the truck. He knew if he offered you punks enough money you'd drive the truck to Washington. It was my job to make sure you got a good look at Jake's body. I also had to make sure you knew we could do the same thing to you and your little girlfriends. We don't even need Jake anymore; we've got a long list of customers. Hell we can't keep up with the demand. We planned to keep operating, just splitting the money three ways. That's another reason we weren't about to quit. The three of us would make a couple million dollars more without Jake. This time I came down to help Mac drive the stuff up north. I've been keeping my truck and boat at Black's place all summer. Every chance I get, I come down here and run the Cigarette up and down the Cape Fear. Man that's one fast boat, I love to open her up and let her fly. You ass holes can have your old fishing boat, give me a speedboat anytime. That's how we got over here tonight, in my boat. It's tied up right behind that piece of junk you fish in. Anyway Mac and me were over at Black's place waiting for him to call us to pick up the dope. Black called and said everything was running late, said the dumb ass fisherman's boat had broke down. He said the fisherman's name was Ray Cook. He said if Cooks trying something stupid he would regret it. He would call us back when the stuff gets there. Black never did call us back. After midnight Mac and me rode by Black's store, his car was gone, and all the lights were off. Then we noticed a police car parked across the street. We knew something was wrong, so we took my truck and boat and went to a motel. Later we heard about this car found on a bridge down here. It sounded like Black's car so we came down here and checked in a motel. We looked your name and address up in the phone book. Later we heard the cops had traced the car to Black, they also raided both of his stores looking for dope. They couldn't find any because there had never been any dope at his Washington store, and you two ass holes have got the dope down here. Mac and me decided to lay low and watch you punks for a while, sometimes in my truck, and sometimes in my boat. We're sure you ain't had time to sell the dope yet. We figure you've got it hid in the house or on the boat. We wanted to see if the cops were watching you, before we made our move. We wanted to make sure the cops weren't just waiting for you to sell the stuff so they could catch your dealer too. We followed you punks all around this place. We even followed your little girlfriends over to their apartment the other day. Man! Those sure are two cute little things. We won't have any trouble finding that place again. Hell! After we kill you two we might pay them a visit just to be polite. While you punks were off screwing all weekend we checked your place over real good. We looked everywhere we could, but we didn't find the dope. You two idiots never even knew anybody had been in your house. I guess you ass holes were feeling pretty good, it doesn't look like the cops are on to you, but I am. You've got our dope around here somewhere, and I intend to get it. You ass holes have put us out of business, but Mac and I can still make enough to retire on from that one package. The cops don't know we were partners with Black, so they've got no reason to look for us. We'll go ahead and deal this last load from my place. Then we'll retire someplace where the sun always shines. I'm getting tired of living in D.C. anyway. I still can't believe you two had balls enough to take on ol Black. Did you kill him before you threw him off the bridge or did you just let the fall do it?"

Ray's body was shaking all over. How could they have been so wrong? They miscalculated everything. The people from Washington knew who they were and had found them. The cops hadn't even raided the right place, so Pete was never arrested. Now he was about to kill them for something they didn't even have. He also knew where the girls lived. What would he do to them later? His worst nightmare was coming true and he was powerless to do anything about it.

Pete said, "Now it's time to tell me where the dope's at."

Ray replied, "If you kill us you'll never find out where it's at."

Pete walked over and sat on the couch beside Ray. He said, "I told you before I was done you'd tell me everything I wanted to know. I'm not going to kill you yet, but I will make you talk."

He pressed the gun in Ray's groin and said, "you'll tell me where the dopes at, or I'll turn you into a woman. Then I'll do the same thing to your brother. Then Mac will go get your little girlfriends, and you can watch us ball hell out of them before Mac takes his knife to their pretty faces. Believe me Mac can do things with a knife that will make them beg to be killed. Now you ready to talk?"

"Ok" replied Ray "you win, you can kill us, but please don't do anything to the girls. They don't know anything about us being in the dope business. I'll tell you everything you want to know. The dope's buried with Black's body out in Green Swamp."

"What the hell is Green Swamp?

"It's a big swamp about ten miles from here. We buried Black and the dope out there."

"You expect me to believe that crap. Everybody knows Black was fed to the fish, and nobody's stupid enough to bury a couple million dollars worth of dope."

"It's true," said Joe "I shot Black with an arrow then we buried him and the dope out in the swamp. Then we put his car on the high-rise bridge, so everybody would think he jumped off the bridge and killed himself. If his body were ever found the cops would know he had been shot with an arrow and start a murder investigation. We didn't know where to sell the dope and we just wanted out of the mess, so we threw it in the hole with Black's body."

Pete looked at Mac and said, "It's hard to believe, but these two just might be stupid enough to do something like that. What do you think we ought to do?"

Mac finally spoke, "if the dopes in the swamp then let's go get it. After we get the dope we can kill these two and leave their bodies out there. We'll be back in D.C. before anybody even knows they're missing. Hell they might never be found."

"Ok, ass holes, what do we need to get the dope out," said Pete.

"Two shovels and two flashlights," replied Ray "I'll have to drive my truck, you can't get there without a four-wheel drive."

"Bullshit" said Pete "I'll drive."

Ray replied, "have you ever driven a truck in a swamp before? If you don't know what you're doing we'll be stuck up before we're half way there. The roads like one big mud hole."

Pete thought a minute then said, "ok you drive, but I'll have my gun in your ribs the whole way."

Ray answered "you'll have to uncuff me so I can change the gears. Then we'll get the stuff we'll need to get the dope out. The flashlights are in the kitchen and the shovels are in the garage."

Mac walked over and took the cuffs off of Ray. Then he followed him as he got two flashlights and two shovels and put them in his truck. Then Ray got behind the wheel with Pete beside him, and Joe and Mac got in the back. Ray cranked the truck and they headed for Green Swamp. He was thinking, if they could just get in the swamp the guys might have a chance. He had noticed both Pete and Mac were wearing boat shoes while he and Joe both had on boots. At least that would slow them down a little. That might give the brothers a chance to make a run for it. He and Joe knew the swamp as well as anyone. He was betting Pete and Mac had never been in a swamp, especially at night. They had no idea what was waiting for them. Anything could happen in a swamp.

CHAPTER 11

Ray drove up the paved road and turned onto the same dirt road he had the week before. Neither he nor Pete had said a word during the drive to the swamp. Pete had his pistol poked in his ribs so hard they were beginning to get sore. They headed deep into the swamp. The ride was so rough Ray was afraid Pete‘s gun might go off by mistake.

“Damn ass hole,” growled Pete “I knew I should have drove. Do you have to hit every bump and mud puddle out here? I think you’re driving like hell just trying to scare us, but you’re just wasting your time. Nothing scares us you punk.

“This is a swamp,” replied Ray “it’s not an interstate highway. You have to expect to be tossed around a little going down a road like this. It’ll get a lot worst before we get there.”

Just like the last time they continued to drive deeper and deeper into the swamp. Ray could hear Joe and Mac being tossed around in the back of the truck. Mac was cussing up a storm. The whole situation would have been funny if he wasn’t so worried about what would happen later. Ray finally stopped the truck at the same spot he had stopped when they had brought Black’s body out.

“We’ll have to walk from here,” he said

“Wait a minute, ass hole, you didn’t say nothing about tramping around in the swamp,” shouted Pete.

“You don’t think we buried him beside the road do you. We carried him way out in the swamp, so nobody would ever find him. We might even have a hard time finding him ourselves.”

“Don’t try to pull that crap on us,” growled Pete “I think you ass holes know exactly where he’s at. We ought to go ahead and blow one of you away right now. We don’t need but one to find the stuff.”

“I‘m telling you we hid Black real good. Even with both of us looking his grave’s going to be hard to find.”

“All right, let’s go out in the damn swamp,” growled Pete “I hope you’ve got enough sense not to try any funny business. I’m already pissed off enough to blow you away. My clothes cost a bundle of money, and I‘m going to ruin them in this damn swamp. These damn shoes cost over five hundred dollars. I swear, the first gator I see, I'm going to plug you and give him a nice lunch.”

"All I can say is if we run into some of the dangerous animals in this place you'd better shoot them and not me," replied Ray "they'll go after anything that moves."
The four of them got the lights and shovels and got out of the truck.

Ray said, “I’m telling you guys this is going to be a long and difficult walk. You can expect to slip and slid all over the place. You’re also going to get cut up by all the thorns and briars. Joe and I are still all scratched up from our last trip out here. If you want the dope bad enough a little pain shouldn’t bother you.”

“Just shut the hell up and get moving,” replied Pete.

Once more the brothers went walking through the swamp, in the middle of the night. This time was different: this time they probably wouldn't be coming back. Ray went first, with a flashlight in his left hand and a shovel in his right. Next came Pete, with his gun at Ray's back. Then came Joe, with his hands still cuffed, carrying a shovel. Last was Mac, with a light in his left hand and a gun in his right. The mud and muck was ankle deep. Just like when they had brought Black's body out here, the going was very rough. Five mornings ago they had dragged Black's body through the swamp. Now you couldn't tell anyone had ever been there. The swamp had quickly erased all signs of human activity. Ray could feel the mud and muck coming in his boots. He had to smile just thinking about what Pete and Mac were feeling. They hadn't walked far before they had to stop; the muck had pulled one of Mac's shoes off.

"Damn this crap," growled Pete "if you ass holes are trying anything stupid I'm going to blow your brains all over this damn swamp."

"The dopes out here, I guarantee that," said Ray "you can see how hard it is moving around in this place. Just imagine how hard it was dragging Black's body through this crap. We might have to look around for a while before we find his grave. We did our best to hide it. Even if it were day light it would be hard to find."

"This is like walking around in a bunch of shit." Shouted Mac "You punks hurry up and find the stuff so we can get the hell out of this crap. If we're out here much longer, I'm going to start blowing things off.

"We've got a lot farther to go," replied Joe "we carried his body out in the swamp until we just couldn't go any farther. It sure wasn't easy."

"This is bullshit," exclaimed Mac "we should have just waited in the truck until it got light."

"You two are in such a big hurry to get the dope you wouldn't wait for anything. Besides I'm sure you'd rather kill us while it's still dark."

"If I spend much more time sliding around in this damn swamp, it ain't going to matter how dark it is; I'm going to fill you full of lead."

They continued slipping and sliding through the swamp, having to stop often for Pete and Mac to put a shoe back on. Each time they stopped Ray noticed that Joe and Mac were dropping a little farther behind. They walked right over Black's grave and kept going. Joe kept his mouth shut. He figured since they had gone over Black's grave Ray was planning something. He tried to keep Ray in his sight all the time. Ray wasn't sure what he was going to do. If nothing else he would get Pete and Mac so deep in the swamp they would never find their way out. Joe and Mac were at least ten feet behind Ray and Pete. They were about two hundred feet from Black's grave when they came to a big tree laying in the way. Ray stepped over it with his right foot and was about to bring his left foot over when he saw something that sent a chill down his spine. On a tree limb right in front of him laid a four-foot long cottonmouth water moccasin. He was sure Pete hadn't seen it. Ray brought his other foot over the tree, bent low, and dropped the shovel. He knew the snake would be easy to catch, it was about time for them to hibernate, and they were sluggish in the cool weather. He grabbed the snake behind its head. Then he turned and held the light as Pete put one foot over the tree. There was no way Pete could see what he held in his right hand. When Pete brought his other foot over the tree Ray threw the snake at him and yelled "cottonmouth." The snake hit Pete on the shoulder and sank its deadly fangs in his neck. Pete was so surprised he screamed and fell back against the tree. He dropped his gun in his lap as he grabbed for his neck and threw the snake off him. Ray threw the light to his left and took off running to his right. When Mac heard Pete scream he shined his light forward to see what was happening. Joe turned and hit him on the side of his head with the shovel. Then he took off through the swamp. Although pretty dazed, Mac managed to hold on to the light and his gun. He tried to catch Joe in the light and fired a couple of bullets in his direction. Joe vanished in the swamp.

Pete was screaming, “The damn snake bit me. The damn snake bit me.”
Mac was still kind of woozy. He took out his handkerchief and pressed it against the gash in his head. Then he staggered up to Pete and asked, “where’d he bite you at?”

“He bit me in the damn neck,” screamed Pete “Mac you got to do something. You got to help me. Mac, Please do something. I can already feel the poison going through my body.”
Mac shined the light on Pete’s neck. He could see two small punctures with a little blood dripping from them. Pete’s neck was already starting to swell up.

“What the hell can I do? I don’t know anything about a snakebite. Besides I‘ve got a big gash on the side of my head. Joe hit me with the damn shovel. My head feels like it going to explode. If I bend over I‘ll probably pass out.”

“Please Mac,” begged Pete “please do something to help me. I don’t want to die.”

“You’re in the middle of a swamp, in the middle of the night, and you just got bit by a poisonous snake. What the hell do you want me to do? I just want to get out of this place alive. Right now, I ain‘t even worried about the dope anymore. I just want to get out of this damn swamp.”

"Please Mac, you got to help me. Please, pleaseeee, Pete's throat had swollen shut. He leaned his head back against the tree and tried to breathe. Less than a minute later he was dead. Mac started shining the light all around the swamp. There was no chance of him seeing Ray or Joe.

Meanwhile Ray was trying to work his way back to Joe. He didn't know if he had been shot or even if he was still alive. There was just enough moonlight for him to see about three feet in front of him. He could always tell where Mac was by just looking at his light. Ray had gone a short distance when he heard a whisper, "that you Ray?"

"Yeah" he whispered back "you all right Joe?"

"Yeah" answered Joe "Mac took a few shots at me but he missed. Let's just keep talking softly and follow each other's voice. I hit Mac on the head with the shovel. He's got to be in a lot of pain now."

Ray answered, "the cottonmouth bit Pete in the neck. He won't last long if he's not already dead."

Finally the brothers were together.

"At least we're both still alive," said Joe.

"Thank God," answered Ray "now we've got to figure out a way to get Mac."

Suddenly Mac turned his light off.

"Damn" said Ray "he's smarter than I thought he was. He knows as long as he has the light on we know exactly where he's at. Plus he's not burning up the batteries."

Joe said, "If we could find our way back to the truck we could go home and come back with our guns."

"It won't be easy without a light, but it's the best chance we've got," replied Ray "I know we walked over Black's grave about two hundred feet back. Let's start making our way toward it."

Slowly the brothers started walking toward where they thought Black was buried. If they could get that far the rest of the way back to the truck wouldn't be nearly as hard. Ray led while Joe, who still had on cuffs, held on to his shirt. It wasn't an easy walk in the dark. There was no way to see all the brush, and limbs, and they kept slapping them in the face. With every step they could feel the thorns and briars tear at their flesh. They were already pretty well scratched up, so they were getting new scratches on top of old ones. Both men continuously slid down in the mud and muck. With no light to see what was in front of him, Ray had to take very short steps. There was always the danger of stepping in a sinkhole or on a snake or gator. Plus they had to move as silently as possible, they sure didn't want Mac to see or hear them. They looked back often to make sure he hadn't turned on his light. Every now and then the light would flick on and then right back off. Ray figured Mac was checking out every noise he heard. After what seemed like an hour Ray whispered, "I think this is Black's grave I'm standing on. It should be a lot better going from here on."

The brothers were pretty good at directions; after all they used to poach deer in the swamp at night. They continued heading in the direction they thought the truck was in. It was a slow and tiring trip, but they finally made out the shadow of the truck. They walked over to it and took a minute to catch their breath. Then Ray got behind the wheel and Joe got in the passenger side.

"Mac might hear the truck when we leave, sound carries pretty good in the swamp," remarked Ray " I'm sure he's still back at Pete's body waiting for daylight, there's no way he could get here to stop us."

Ray cracked up the truck and backed it up until he found a place to turn it around. Then he drove out of the swamp and headed for Oak Island. As they were going down the road he said, "I can't believe this is happening. Please tell me it's all a bad dream."

"I'm afraid its real," replied Joe "and I've just thought about something else we've got to do. Pete said he drove his boat over to our place. We've got to get rid of that boat before it gets light. It's the only thing that can connect us to Pete and Mac."

"You're right, we sure don't want anybody to see their boat parked at our pier. I know what to do, we'll take it way out in the ocean and sink it. It'll take some time but we've got to do it. You drive the Cigarette, and I'll follow you in the Carolina. We've got to hurry; it's going to be daylight before long. We'll have to get rid of the boat before we come back for Mac."

"Ok, when we get home do something about these cuffs. Then I can drive the Cigarette. If Pete took the keys we'll have to hot-wire it."

Ray pulled his truck into the driveway, and both of them went into the garage. Then he took a hammer and chisel and broke the chain on the cuffs. At least now Joe had both of his hands free. They walked out to the Cigarette and checked the ignition switch. There were no keys in it.

"I'll check the glove compartment," Ray said "sometimes people keep an extra key in there."

Ray opened the compartment and moved its contents around; sure enough there was an extra boat key. He put the key in the switch and cranked the boat up.

"This baby sure sounds sweet" he said "I'd love to open her up one time just to see what she'd do. I guess I'll never know. Ok Joe; take her way out in the ocean. Just don't go to fast, the Carolina can't keep up with this boat."

Joe got behind the wheel, backed the Cigarette around, and slowly headed the boat down the canal. Ray was right behind him in the Carolina. They got to the waterway and headed out to sea. There wasn't another boat in sight. The water was as calm as Ray had ever seen it. That would help them make good time. They got to the two-mile buoy and kept going. They got to the four-mile buoy and kept going. They would make sure nobody ever found the Cigarette. They went out farther, and farther, farther than Ray had ever fished. They were at least twelve miles out when Joe cut the cigarette's engine. Ray pulled the Carolina up beside the Cigarette and shined his spotlight on Joe. Joe raised the boat's engine cover and screwed the plug out of the boat's bottom. Then he stepped over to the Carolina. Water began rushing into the Cigarette. The brothers watched as the boat filled with water and sank beneath the waves. They could see it a few feet below the surface as it headed for the bottom of the ocean.

"It's a damn shame to have to sink such a nice boat," said Joe "but we had to do it. I'll bet ol Pete had to sell a whole bunch of dope to buy that boat."

"Yeah" said Ray "I couldn't even guess how much that boat cost. One things for sure though, nobody will ever find her way out here. Now we'd better hurry back, the sun's starting to come up."

It was nearly daylight when they pulled up to their pier. They had been up all night and they were bone tired but they couldn't stop now. Mac was still in the swamp, they had to find him and finish him off, sleep would have to wait. They went in the house and Ray got his pistol while Joe got his 30-30 rifle. Both men got plenty of ammunition. If Mac put up a fight, they would be ready. Then they got back in the truck and headed for Green Swamp. There was no need to talk; both men knew what they had to do. They also knew things would look a lot different in the daylight. Ray drove down the dirt road and stopped the truck at the same spot they had left a few hours ago. They got out of the truck and looked around. The swamp seemed deadly silent in the daylight.

"We don't have any idea where Mac is," he said "I hope he's still at Pete's body. It won't be hard to find that spot again. We'll have to walk just like we were stalking deer."

Ray started moving as silently as possible through the swamp. Joe followed about fifty feet behind him.

They had hunted deer this way many times. Walking in the swamp was a lot easier in the daytime. It didn't take long to reach Black's grave; they had been there enough times to know the way. Ray stopped there and waited for Joe to catch up. There was no sign of Mac anywhere.

"Well" said Ray "hopefully he's still at Pete's body. It's only about two hundred feet from here. Maybe we should spread out and approach it from different directions."

"That's a good idea," replied Joe "I'll go about a hundred feet west and come in from that direction. Give me twenty minutes before you start moving."

Joe turned right and started walking; he was soon out of sight. Ray waited twenty minutes than began moving slowly toward Pete's body. He moved as silently as possible, if Mac was there he wanted to catch him by surprise. It took a while, but he finally saw the big tree where they had left Pete. There was still no sign of Mac. He could be hiding behind the tree thought Ray. He moved around to his left to where he was at the end of the tree. He could see Pete's body, but there was no sign of Mac. As he moved toward Pete's body, Joe appeared from the other end of the tree.

"I didn't see any sign of Mac at all," he whispered

"Me neither," replied Ray "let me check in Pete's pockets and see if there's a key for those cuffs."

He felt in Pete's pants pockets and pulled out a key. He took it and opened the cuffs on each of Joe's wrist.

"That feels much better," said Joe "My wrists are about raw."

"I wonder if Mac tried to move while it was still dark or waited for day light," said Ray

"If he has any sense he waited for daylight. If he moved in the dark he might be in a sinkhole full of quicksand. If he is he'll never be found, and we'll never know if he's dead or not. Let's spread out and walk a couple hundred feet out in the swamp looking for him. Let's meet back here in an hour. Then if we haven't found Mac we'll go ahead and bury Pete."

The guys started moving farther into the swamp. An hour later they were both back at Pete's body. Neither of them had seen a sign of Mac.

“We can’t search the whole swamp looking for Mac,” said Ray “let’s go ahead and bury Pete.”

Pete’s body was still sitting against the tree with his pistol on his lap.

“I saw a spot about fifty feet south of here that's clear enough to dig in,” said Joe.

“Ok, my shovels laying right where I left it. Let’s see if we can find yours.”

Ray picked up his shovel and they went back to where Joe had dropped his. It wasn’t hard to find; there was still a little of Mac’s blood on it.

“Ha! I hit that sucker good,” laughed Joe “I hope I killed the son of a bitch. You reckon a gators already drug his body off somewhere?”

“I hope he’s dead, but we need to find his body. That’s the only way we’ll know for certain. If we don‘t find him we‘ll always wonder if he‘ll catch up with us some day.”

The brothers made their way to the spot Joe had seen. They decided only one would dig and the other would keep a watch for Mac. They would trade places every fifteen minutes. It took a while but they finally had a hole about six feet deep. They walked back to Pete’s body. Ray picked up Pete’s pistol and put it under his belt, then they rolled him over and took all the money out of his wallet. Next each brother grabbed one of Pete’s arms and started dragging him toward the hole.

“At least he’s not as heavy as Black was,” said Joe

“Yeah, and we don’t have to drag him nearly as far as we did Black. Being able to see where we‘re walking sure helps a lot.”

They got to the hole and threw Pete’s body in it. Ray threw his pistol on his chest.

“We don’t want any sign of him left behind,” he said

They took turns filling the hole with dirt and watching for Mac. When the hole was full they covered it with leaves and pine needles. When they finished it looked the same as Black's grave; just a mound of dirt.

"Well that's the second body we've buried in this swamp," said Ray "you reckon we should say something over ol Pete's grave?"

"OK" replied Joe "how about this: Lord I sure hope it didn't kill that poor snake when he bit this sorry son of a bitch in the neck."

"You just can't be serious can you. I guess we'd better both get serious because Macs still out here somewhere. We've got to make sure he's dead before we leave this swamp."

"What do we do now? We could spend a month out here looking for him and never find him."

"I don't know," replied Ray "I'm too tired to think. The chances of Mac getting out of the swamp are slim. Maybe we should go back to the truck and get some rest. Maybe after dark we'll be able to see his light, if he's anywhere around here. We can take turns sleeping in the back of the truck."

"We need to make sure he's dead, or we'll always be looking behind our backs," replied Joe "but I've got to have some rest to. Let's head back to the truck."

With their guns in one hand and a shovel in the other, the brothers started walking toward the truck. They moved a little faster going back; it didn't look like Mac was anywhere around. With any luck he was already dead. They seemed to get their second wind just thinking about getting some rest. They were a few feet from the truck when they heard a booming voice say, "hold it right there you two."

The brothers froze; standing on the other side of the truck was Mac with his pistol pointed right at them.

“Drop those guns and shovels, and walk on over and put your hands on the hood of the truck,” Mac shouted.

They both did what Mac had told them to do.

“Well, well, look at what I just found,” laughed Mac “I guess you two ass holes thought the swamp had done ate me up by now. I’ve got a lot more sense than you think I’ve got. I could hear your truck when you left this morning. Sound carries real good in this mud hole. I started walking in this direction. I knew eventually I’d find the road; although, it’s hard to tell this is a road. I came out about a quarter of a mile farther up and just waited. I knew you would come back with guns. There’s no way you could leave me alive. You took longer than I thought you would. I guess you got rid of the boat while you were gone. It’s the only thing that can connect you and me. Anyway I heard your truck when you drove in. I walked back to it and waited for you to come back. I figured after you couldn’t find me, and had buried Pete, you’d come on back from that direction. What else could you do? You could have searched the swamp forever and not found me. You didn't really think I'd be stupid enough to just wait for you at Pete's body, did you? Ok, so much for the chitchat, I’ve had it with you two. I should go ahead and blow one of you away right now. Especially you Joe, my damn heads been throbbing all night. I’m really going to enjoy killing you, yeah; I’m really going to enjoy it. I might not be able to wait until we get to the dope. Here’s what we’re going to do; you lead me straight to the dope, no funny business. When I get the dope, I’ll kill you two and drive the truck back to Washington. If I don’t get the dope, I’ll still kill you two and leave you out here. Then

I'll go get your cute little girlfriends. You don't even want to think about what I'll do to them. Let's just say I'll have some fun before I use my knife on them. Just think about those pretty little necks being sliced open from ear to ear. There's no way you two are getting out of here alive. It's up to you whether your little girlfriends die or not. Frankly all I want to do is kill you ass holes and get the hell back to Washington. I need a doctor to fix up my head. If you two cooperate with me, I'm willing to let your little girls live. Now you two ready to get me the dope."

"Ok," said Ray "we'll do anything you say. You can kill us, but please leave the girls alone. We'll take you to the dope."

"No tricks this time," shouted Mac "I swear I'll blow one of you away. There's one more thing, my feet are raw, what size boots you two got on?"

"Nine and a half," replied Ray

"Ten" said Joe.

"Ok," Mac said "Joe you and me are going to trade. Both of you walk to the back of the truck."

When they got to the back of the truck Mac told Ray to lay on the ground and put his hands behind him. Then he had Joe open the tailgate and take off his boots. After that he made Joe lay on the ground next to Ray. Mac sat on the tailgate and put the boots on. Then he threw his shoes at Joe.

"Here you can wear these sorry things," he said "I hope your feet get as raw as mine are. OK, get up, and grab the shovels, and let's go. My trigger finger's real itchy and I don't give a damn about killing one of you, so you'd better take me straight to the dope. No bullshit this time."

"I'll lead," said Ray "just follow me Joe. It's going to be a long walk Mac, so don't get too impatient. At least this time we can see where we're going."

"Well let's get the damn show on the road" replied Mac.

The guys got their shovels and started walking back into the swamp. This time they had to stop ever now and then for Joe to put on a shoe. That was all right with Mac, he didn't want to go very fast anyway. Each time the guys got over three feet in front of him he shouted for them to slow down. Nothing was going to go wrong this time. This could work out great he thought; I'll have all the dope money by myself. After I sell it I'll have enough to last me the rest of my life. I'll leave D.C. and move someplace nice, maybe Florida or Jamaica. Anywhere it doesn't get to cold. It's to bad all my partners had to get themselves killed and leave all the money to me.

Joe was thinking about his life. When they were in the swamp last night he always thought there was a chance he and Ray could get away. Now it was daylight; Mac could always keep both brothers in sight. Last night a miracle had saved him and Ray. He couldn't count on another miracle. He had to face the fact that he was going to die. Mac was itching to kill him anyway. The gash on Mac's head looked pretty bad. He was probably telling the truth about killing the brothers and hurrying back to Washington. At least the girls would be safe. Joe realized he had only one real regret; he should have married Mona a long time ago. He thought they had plenty of time. He now realized that nobody really knows how much time they have in the world. In a short while his body would be left in the swamp. Mona would never know what happened to him. Would she worry herself sick wondering where he was? He said a quick prayer: God please comfort her during the next couple of months. Please let someone find my body so she'll at least know I'm dead. I sure don't want her to think I just ran out on her. As soon as he muttered the words he had a horrible thought: nobody would ever find his or Ray's bodies. After Mac killed them, and left the swamp, the gators would move in. They'd gorge themselves right away, then take anything left over back to their lairs to eat at their leisure. It almost made him sick just thinking about being gator food.

Ray wasn't ready to give up. He was busy thinking of a plan to get Mac. There was a slim chance he and Joe could get out alive. If nothing else he was determined to get Mac so lost in the swamp he would never find his way out. He got a little satisfaction knowing that Mac would face a slow death trying to find his way out of Green Swamp. With the exception of Jake, everybody that was involved in the dope scheme would end up in Green Swamp forever.

They continued walking through the swamp. It was amazing how different everything looked in the daytime. Being able to see where they were going certainly made walking a lot easier. Ray and Joe had been here in the daylight before, Mac hadn't. There had to be some way to use that to their advantage. First they headed south, and then Ray seemed to make a very slow turn toward the west. Mac seemed unaware of what direction they were going in. He was just following Ray. Joe just kept quiet; he knew Ray would ask if he needed his help finding the way. They walked around in the swamp for a long time before Ray stopped and pointed to a mound of dirt in front of him.

"This is it," he said "this is where we buried Black and the dope."

"It's about damn time," growled Mac "which end of the grave is the dope in?"

"We just threw everything in together," replied Joe "the dope could be anywhere in the hole. It might even be under Black's body. You have to remember it was pitch dark when we did it."

Mac shouted back, "Ray you start digging at one end and Joe you dig at the other end. Don't even dream of trying anything funny, I'll have my gun on you all the time." Ray started digging where he was, and Joe walked a few feet and started to dig. Neither of the brothers said a word as they dug deeper and deeper in the hole. The sun was up high now and it was very hot. Both brothers were soon drenched in sweat. They had been digging about twenty minutes when Joe said,

"How about letting us take a break. We've been up all night and we've both about had it."

"Just keep digging," replied Mac "just remember now that you've led me to the dope I don't need but one of you. I don't care which one of you I kill first. Although I'm really going to enjoy killing you, Joe. My damn head is still throbbing like a son of a bitch. You don't need to worry about rest; you'll both soon be getting an eternal rest." Both brothers continued to dig while Mac watched them, moving his gun from one to the other. They were down about four feet when Ray said,

"We're getting close, I can feel the body, we better start digging with our hands now. If we hit the package with a shovel it might bust open and spill some coke out."

Mac was getting anxious now, "I don't care how you dig, just get the dope out, and you damn sure better not waste any of it" he shouted.

The brothers got down on their hands and knees and started scooping dirt out of the grave. Before long they could make out the outline of a man beneath them. Feeling around in the dirt Ray finally found what he had been searching for. I can't let Mac know he thought, I've got to do something to distract him. Suddenly he stood up and said, "I've got to stretch: my legs are going to sleep."

"Get back to digging," shouted Mac "it won't be long before your whole body's asleep."

As Ray kneeled down he whispered to Joe, "I've found it, give me a minute, then get Mac's attention."

Both of them went back to scooping out dirt. With his right hand under the dirt Ray got a good grip on the object he had found. If his plan didn't work he knew both he and Joe would be dead men.

About that time Joe shouted to Mac, "I feel something soft down here, I think I've found the package."

Mac was clearly excited; he walked toward Joe and leaned over the hole. Ray had his back toward Joe. He suddenly raised his hand out of the dirt, turned around, pointed a pistol at Mac, and pulled the trigger. Bam, bam, bam three slugs hit Mac in the chest. He staggered backward a few feet and fell on his back. The brothers looked out of the hole at his body. He lay perfectly still. Joe climbed out of the hole and walked over to him. Mac's chest was covered with blood, no doubt about it, he was dead. Ray climbed out of the hole and walked over beside Joe.

Joe said, "Ol Mac never knew what hit him. He had no idea this was Pete's grave instead of Black's. He thought he was going to get the dope, but he got three slugs instead. How did you ever think of such a brilliant plan?"

“I had time to think while I was lying on the ground,” replied Ray “I deliberately walked around in the swamp, so Mac would be totally lost. If he had killed us, I don’t think he would have ever found his way out of the swamp. I knew Mac would never recognize Black’s grave. It was dark when we walked over it, and everything looks different in the daylight. We moved Pete’s body away from the tree, so I knew Mac had no idea where he was at. I remembered throwing Pete’s gun on his chest, but I wasn’t even sure I could find his grave. I couldn’t walk straight to it. I had to make sure Mac was good and lost before I started looking for it. I was just praying the gun would fire when the time came.”

“Well the swamp has another victim,” Joe said “let me get me boots off of him, and we’ll throw him in the hole with Pete.”

Joe bent down and took his boots off of Mac’s feet. While he was putting them on Ray cleaned all the money out of Mac’s billfold. Then they pulled his body over to the hole and dropped him in, along with both guns, his shoes, and billfold. Then they filled the hole with dirt and covered it with leaves and pine needles. Of course when they finished it looked like nothing but a big mound of dirt.

“Well” said Ray “there’s three bodies buried out here and nobody knows it but us. We don’t have to worry about anybody ever finding them. This time I want to say something over the grave. Lord thank you for leading me to Pete‘s grave, and thank you for letting that gun shoot when I needed it to. Please let this be the last man we ever kill.”

“Amen” said Joe “by the way Lord: if there’s a particularly hot place in hell make sure you send these three to it.”

“If you can’t be serious then let’s just get the hell out of here,” replied Ray.

Once more the brothers made their way out of the swamp. They were in no hurry this time. They weren't worried about anybody looking for them. They were too tired to move fast anyway. They found their way to the truck, cranked it up, and headed for Oak Island. While driving down the road Ray said, "you think anybody else will come looking for us?"

"I don't know," answered Joe "the only names we heard mentioned were Black, Pete, Mac, and Jake and they're all dead. Somebody might have been in on it that we didn't hear of. We'll have to keep looking behind our backs as long as we stay here. Frankly I've had enough. It's time for us to move away, maybe even change our names. How much money have we got in the safe?"

"Two hundred and eighty thousand dollars"

"That works out to a hundred and forty grand each. How much can we sell the house for?"

"The house ain't fancy, but it sets on prime real estate, and has lots of privacy. We should be able to get between two and two hundred fifty grand for it. It might take a while to sell it though."

"We've both got a little in the bank, and you can sell the boat. We've got enough money to give us a nice start some place new."

"I'm ready to go," replied Ray "I'm sure we can get the girls to go with us. Let's try to get a little sleep and go see the girls at the usual time. We'll talk some more after we get some rest."

CHAPTER 12

When they got home the guys cleaned up, then each went to his bedroom and tried to sleep. Both managed to get little catnaps between plenty of tossing and turning. After a couple of hours they both got up and took a shower. Feeling much better they sat at the kitchen table again.

Ray said, “I’ve been thinking about something that’ll be pretty neat. I want to pull a big surprise on the girls. Let’s take them to Myrtle Beach tomorrow and get married.”

“That’s a great idea,” replied Joe “I’m sure they’ll love it.”

“There’s one more thing I want to run by you. When we get married why don’t we take the girls last names instead of them taking ours. That way we’ll have our names changed to. Ray and Joe Cook will cease to exist. When we move away we won’t leave a forwarding address so nobody will know where we’re living. When we begin our new lives we can tell people we’re half brothers.”

“That’ll be ok with me, the girls will be tickled to death.”

“I’ll go ahead, and call a realtor, and see about putting the house on the market,” said Ray “after we’re married let’s take the girls on a nice honeymoon. I’d like to check out the mountains. I know it’s beautiful up there at this time of the year. That might be a real nice place to move to.”

“Great” replied Joe “get out your best suit. Something nice enough to get married in. I can‘t wait to see the look on both the girls faces.”

The brothers were at the girl’s apartment right after they got home from work. The girls should have known something was up by the sheepish grin of each of the guy’s faces.

Joe said, “Let’s all go sit at the kitchen table. There’s something we want to ask you.”

The four of them went into the kitchen and sat down at the table.

Then Ray said, “How would you girls like to go to Myrtle Beach tomorrow morning and get married?”

What a surprise, neither girl was expecting anything like that. They looked at each other and smiled. Then both answered with a loud, “yes.”

Carol said, “but what about our jobs? Both of us have to work tomorrow.”

“Call them in the morning and tell them you quit,” said Ray “you both hate those jobs anyway. After we’re married we want to find someplace new to move to. Sort of have a new beginning. Joe has already quit his job and I’m tired of working on the boat. We just want to go somewhere new and start over; you wouldn’t mine doing that would you?”

Carol said, “if that’s what you want to do it’s fine with me. As long as we’re together I’m happy.”

“That goes for me too,” said Mona as she looked at Joe.

Joe said, “Let me tell you what else we want to do. When we get married we want to take your last names. We’re really modern men and besides we’ve always liked your last names.”

“Great day!” said Mona “you mean you would give up your last name for us.”

“Darn right we would,” said Joe

“But you’re brothers,” replied Carol “how can you have a different last name?”

“Don’t worry,” said Ray “we’ll just tell people we’re half brothers. It’s nobody else's business anyway. When we move away nobody‘s going to know the difference. Just make sure you never use our old last name.”

The girls were tickled pink. Not only were they getting married but also their men were willing to take their last names. How in the world could they be so lucky?

Joe said, “After we get married tomorrow we'll go on a nice honeymoon. How would you girls like to go to the mountains?”

“That’s fine with me,” said Mona “it’s been at least ten years since I visited the mountains. This is the perfect time to go there. All the leaves are changing colors.”

“That sounds great” remarked Carol, “ this is all so wonderful I need to pinch myself to make sure I‘m not dreaming.”

“This is not a dream baby,” said Ray “this is what I’ve been wanting to do for a long time.”

“What about your families,” remarked Joe “Have you had a chance to talk to them yet?”

“Not yet,” replied Mona “but that's sure not going to stop me from getting married."

"Don't you at least want to tell them?"

"I'll call my folks and tell them, but I'm sure they won't come on such a short notice."

"I'll call mine too," said Carol "maybe we can stop by home on our way to the mountains."

"Sure" replied Ray "Charlotte is right on our way. We'll stop by and see both of your families. We're going to be real pressed for time tomorrow. We better figure on leaving for our honeymoon the next day. Let's plan on getting to Charlotte around noon the day after tomorrow."

"Our parents are good friends and only live a few blocks from each other," said Mona "I'll see if everyone can get together at Carol's parent's Thursday afternoon."

Suddenly Carol said, "oh my! I don't have any clothes that are nice enough to get married in."

"Me neither," remarked Mona "you guys know we always wear jeans and shirts. We can't get married wearing them. I don't even own a fancy dress."

"Don't worry about it," replied Joe "we'll stop by the mall and get you both a nice dress. You two will be the best looking brides in the country."

"You sure will," said Ray "we feel kind of guilty anyway. You girls deserve a much nicer wedding than we're giving you. You should have all your family and friends watching. If you want to wait and have something fancy we'll understand."

"I've waited long enough," said Carol "I want to get married tomorrow."

"Joe, this is what I dreamed about all the time you were at sea," remarked Mona "I just want to marry you and spend the rest of my life with you. I don't care about a fancy wedding."

The brothers had to take a deep breath and compose themselves. The last few years seemed to flash through each of their minds. This was what it was all about. It was worth all their hard work. Their dreams were finally coming true. The girls had no idea what they had been through and they would never tell them. Just hours ago they had killed a man and buried him in the swamp. Now that all seemed like it happened a hundred years ago.

In fact, for the next minute, nobody in the room could talk. They all just sat there and felt the love around them. Tears were rolling down both girls' cheeks. They each grabbed their man's hand and squeezed it tight.

"Please don't cry," begged Ray "You'll have me all misty eyed in a minute."

"I'm just so happy," replied Carol "these are tears of joy. I don't expect you guys to understand."

The guys understood a lot more than the girls were aware of.

Finally Carol dried her eyes and said, "This all sounds to good to be true, are you guys going to have enough money to do all this?"

Joe chipped in, "we've both been putting a little aside for a long time. On all those long trips at sea I didn't have to spend any money. Plus we're going to sell the house, and Ray's selling the boat. We figure we'll get a good price for the house. Waterfront property on the island is worth a fortune. We'll have enough money."

If the girls only knew everything they wouldn't worry about money. The guys were determined to make them believe all their money was legal.

When they got up the next morning the girls called American Chemical Co and quit their jobs. The guys dressed up in their finest suits. Then they all loaded into Carol's car and headed for Myrtle Beach. Just inside the city they stopped at a mall and each girl found a dress she loved. Then they headed for the marriage license bureau and Justice of the Peace. When they told the clerk about the guys changing their last names instead of the girls he just laughed. He said they'd have to take care of the legal stuff later.

There was a special room in the building for people to change cloths in. The girls went in and freshened up and put on their new dresses. When the brothers saw the girls in their wedding dresses, it took their breath away. They weren't just the best looking brides in the country; they were the best looking brides in the world. Each of them was smiling so much they seemed to light up the room when they walked in. It wasn't fancy, but they had a beautiful ceremony. They even drew a small audience from the people working in the office. Double weddings don't happen very often there. After the ceremony they hurried back to the girls apartment, actually now it was their wife's apartment. The guys had to head back to Oak Island to pack and show the house to the realtor. On the way they stopped by a local boat dealer, and Ray told the owner the Carolina was for sale. The owner was familiar with the boat, he offered Ray about half of its real value. Ray winched but since he was in a hurry to sale, and the dealer was paying cash, he took the offer. The dealer was on the waterway, so he could simply drive the boat over to his place. Then the guys went on home. They still approached the house with caution. Ray took his pistol out as he drove down the driveway. There was no need taking any chances, if anybody else was with Pete and Black they could certainly be here by now. They checked around the house and made sure both doors were locked before they went in. They called the realtor and started packing a few things. An hour later the realtor came and checked the house over. He had a big surprise for the brothers. He said he would ask three hundred and fifty grand for the house and put it on the market right away. Evidently the brothers hadn't checked the price of property on the island lately. With all the new people moving in prices have skyrocketed. Especially on waterfront property that had a little privacy. That's what nearly all the newcomers are looking for.

By the time the brothers returned to the girls apartment they were getting a little tired. They had put in a full day. They had: gone to Myrtle Beach and back, gotten married, sold the Carolina, showed the house to a realtor, and packed a suitcase to take on their honeymoon. They were both glad they had decided to wait a day before they left on their honeymoons. Plus their wives wouldn't have to rush so much. The wedding happened so fast they hadn't had time to pack anything. They would also be able to sleep late the next morning. That night there was plenty of champagne for everyone.

They got up at ten the next morning, threw their bags in the vehicles, and headed for Charlotte. Ray and Carol went in Carol's car, and Joe and Mona took Mona's car. The brothers had never met their wives parents. They didn't know how they would accept them. They were afraid their in-laws would blame them for denying their daughters a special wedding.

All their in-laws would be waiting for them at Carol's parent's house. A few hours later both couples pulled into Carol's parent's driveway. Any fears the brothers had were quickly vanished. They were all met with hugs and kisses. Once they got in the house they found a nice wedding cake waiting for them.

Carol pulled her mom aside and said, “mom I’m so happy I could just break out singing.”

“I can tell,” replied her mom “Mona looks very happy too. I’m so glad for both of you. You two certainly did find some handsome men.”

“They are great looking guys, aren’t they. I just love Ray so much. It won’t be long before we give you some beautiful grandkids.”

Their in-laws had a big laugh when Ray told them he and Joe were going to take their wives last names. This is practically unheard of in the south.

Carol’s dad whispered to Mona’s dad, “I wonder if our son in laws know what they’re doing. A long time ago our families were bitter enemies. I’m sure some of them still hold a grudge today. It’s a damn shame all of them can’t be as friendly as our daughters.”

Mona’s dad replied, “These guys seem like they can handle anything. I don’t believe anybody will give them any crap about their last names.”

Was something going on the guys didn’t know about?

After a couple hours visit, and lot’s of coffee and cake, they all kissed goodbye and the couples headed on their honeymoons. In the fall, when all the leaves are changing colors, few places on earth are as beautiful and peaceful as the North Carolina Mountains. After what they had been through the brothers were definitely ready for some peace. Strange as it seems neither of them had ever been to the mountains. The last time their wives were there was on a field trip in high school. They were all looking forward to seeing natures beautiful canopy as well as spending time together.

They got motel rooms just outside the city of Asheville. It was getting late so they decided to just have supper and call it a day. The next day they all loaded into Carol's car and drove down the Blue Ridge Parkway. Since it was the middle of the week traffic wasn't too bad. Nothing like the bumper to bumper traffic on weekends. Especially when all the leaves are at their peak. After living on the coast all their lives the brothers were kind of awestruck by the height of the mountains. Ray had a weird feeling, like he was in the middle of a giant painting. There was beauty all around him. He found something magical about the whole trip. I could definitely spend the rest of my life up here he thought. They spent the next few days checking out the city and resting by the motel pool. Thankfully the motel had an indoor pool. It was too chilly to be outside wearing nothing but a bathing suit.

Mona made a comment about all the scratches on the brother's arms and legs. Fortunately the guys already had a story made up to explain them.

"We caught two sharks in the net the other day," said Joe "we were determined to get them back in the ocean alive. You wouldn't believe how hard it was getting those rascals out of the boat."

"That's so sweet," said Mona "to think you guys wouldn't even kill a shark. How in the world did Carol and I find such sensitive husbands?"

"We were born to be lovers," laughed Joe.

"That's right," replied Ray "you two will get the benefit of all our love."

Carol leaned over and gave Ray a quick kiss, "we're the luckiest women in the world," she said.

On the fourth day they decided to check out some of the old mountain back roads. Several miles south of the city they drove by an old two story Victorian house. The house had a sign out front that said "for sale or rent."

"That could be a beautiful house," said Carol "let's go back and take a look at it."

"That's the ugliest house I've ever seen," replied Ray "It's painted green."

"We can always repaint it; use your imagination a little. Picture that house painted white with a white fence around it."

"You're driving," replied Ray "if you want to check out that house just turn the car around."

Carol turned the car around and stopped in front of the house. They walked around the outside of the house and peeked in the windows. The girls just loved it; they wanted to see all the rooms inside. They drove to the real estate office and asked the agent about the house.

"Just call me Dave," said the agent "that house is only priced at a hundred grand. It needs a lot of work. It could be a real show place if somebody would fix it up. The owner is willing to rent the place if you'd rather do that."

"Let's go look at the inside of it," replied Ray

Dave got the house key and they followed him back to the house. Upon entering the front door they all realized one thing: the house was really huge. It had a large living room, dining room, modern kitchen, two baths, and two large bedrooms downstairs. Upstairs were four more bedrooms and another bath.

“I love it,” said Carol “Ray can we afford to buy it?”

“Sure” replied Ray “after we sell the house at Oak Island we’ll have enough money to buy it and fix it up.”

The brothers pulled Dave aside and said they needed to talk to him alone.

“We’ve got a house at the beach we’re trying to sell,” said Joe “after we sell it we’ll be able to buy this house. Can we draw up a lease to buy option for about six months?”

“That’ll be no problem,” replied Dave “come back to the office and I’ll draw up the paperwork.”

“One more thing,” said Ray “this house is a surprise for our wives. We want the lease in their names.”

“As long as you’ve got enough money for the first months rent it won’t matter who's name it’s in,” said Dave “when do you want the lease to start?”

“Tomorrow” replied Ray

Fortunately the brothers had enough cash to pay the first month’s rent. An hour later the women signed the lease, and Dave gave them the key. The guys figured by the time the lease was up their new names would be official. They would spend the time fixing up the house.

“Well ladies now we’ve got a house,” said Joe “what do you want to do next?”

“Are you kidding,” replied Mona “we want to go home and move all our stuff up here right away.”

“We sure do,” said Carol.

“But we’re still on our honeymoons,” complained Ray “surely you’re not ready for this to end.”

“After we get moved into that house every day will be a honeymoon,” replied Carol with a big smile.

“I’m sure not going to argue with that.”

The next morning they headed back home to pack. Just before they got to the girl’s apartment they stopped to buy some gas, and Ray bought a newspaper. In it was a story about a white truck and a boat trailer that had been parked at the Oak Island public boat ramp for several days. The police had traced the tag to a Pete Wilcox from Washington D.C. Mr. Wilcox owned a Cigarette boat. Wilcox was registered at a local motel, but no one had seen him for a while. Police believe he may have had a boating accident and been lost at sea. The Coast Guard had been searching for any signs of a wreck, but so far nothing had been found. Ray had to smile; he knew they would never find anything.

The guys left the girls at their apartment and headed home to pack. Ray showed Joe the article in the paper. Both guys got a good laugh out of it.

“Mr. Wilcox is certainly lost,” said Joe “he’s lost somewhere in hell along with Black and Mac. They don‘t even mention anyone being with Pete. I guess nobody misses ol Mac.”

“Mac didn’t seem like the family type,” replied Ray “the people that knew him are probably happy he’s not around anymore.”

The guys had been gone for five days. They figured they still better approach the house with caution. Joe got the pistol out as they drove down the driveway. They checked around the house and made sure both doors were locked. Once they were satisfied it was safe, they went in and started packing. They figured they would rent a U Haul and try to take everything in one trip. While they were packing a car drove down their driveway. Ray grabbed the pistol off of the couch. Both brothers ducked down and peeked out the window. They recognized the real estate agent. He had an older couple with him. The couple was both retired schoolteachers from New Jersey, and they wanted to move to the southern coast. They loved the place, especially the privacy of the lot. They made a firm offer of three hundred and fifty thousand dollars, and to top it off they were ready to pay right away. They wanted to move in as soon as the brothers left. They all went to the real estate office and signed the papers. This would be the brother's last official act as Ray and Joe Cook. Since it was getting late the guys went on over to their wife's apartment. They were up bright and early the next morning. They rented a U Haul, and headed for the island, with Joe driving the U Haul and Ray in his truck. The guys just couldn't believe everything was going so good. It was getting tiring, but they checked around the house one more time before they went in. They figured if anybody else were looking for them they would have been here by now. This was their last trip to the house and they couldn't wait to leave. As soon as he got in the house, Ray went in the den and dug out the safe. He replaced all the stones so nobody would ever know there was a hiding place under them. Then he locked the safe in the cab of his truck. They got everything worth taking in the U Haul. They dropped the key by the real estate office and said good-bye to Oak Island.

. They drove to their wives apartment and helped them pack stuff in the U Haul. Between Ray's truck, the U Haul, and the women's cars they managed to get everything loaded in one trip. They were all tired so they spent one last night in the apartment. The next morning they headed for their new home and new life. The plan was to work on the house while waiting for their new name's to become official. The guys would use some of the dope money and pay cash for all the building materials. The women would look for jobs while everybody worked on the house, but there was no hurry. The guys had enough money to last a long time. When they opened an account at the bank for the house and boat money, they put in some of their dope money. They each got a safety deposit box and put the rest of their money in them. They hated to hide it from their wives, but they had no way to explain it. When the lease ran out they would use the money to pay cash for the house. Their wives were so happy they left all the finances to the guys, no questions asked.

The brothers would never return to Oak Island or Green Swamp. They made a pack to never talk about Green Swamp. They were the only ones who knew what had happened there and that's how it would stay. The whole episode seemed like a bad dream. They talked themselves into a rational explanation for their actions. Everyone who died deserved to die. Their only real crime was bringing drugs into the country. To counteract that, they had shut down a group of drug dealers. Their good deeds had overcome their bad ones. They went to bed every night with a clean conscience.

Day by day they worried less about anybody finding them. The only names their neighbors knew were their new names, and they had left no forwarding address at the island. They told their wives to never mention their old names to anyone. That was all in the past, and all they wanted to think about were the present and the future. Maybe one day they would regret what they had did but for now life was great.

By the way, it took a while, but their new names finally became official. Ray's full name became Raymond Michael Lee and Joe's full name became Joseph Leonard Grant. They had often kidded the girls about their last names. Lee and Grant being best friends. Strange as it seemed Carol could trace her ancestors all the way back to General Robert E. Lee, and Mona could trace hers back to Ulysses S. Grant. There was no reason for their in-laws to worry about the brothers taking their wives last names. They were proud of their names.

Just like the brothers had a bond between them so did their wives. It was almost like they were telling the world, no matter who your ancestors were or what they had done, people could still be friends. They had been best friends since they first met in grade school. So today somewhere in the North Carolina Mountains, in a beautiful old house, lives two very happy couples. Mr. and Mrs. Raymond Michael Lee and Mr. and Mrs. Joseph Leonard Grant.

www.ingramcontent.com/pod-product-compliance
Ingram Content Group UK Ltd.
Pitfield, Milton Keynes, MK11 3LW, UK
UKHW041941190726
13854UKWH00004B/1721

9 781411 617476